TRAIL OF THE HUNTER

TRAIL OF THE HUNTER

Dudley Dean

Chivers Press
Bath, England • G.K. Hall & Co.
Thorndike, Maine USA

This Large Print edition is published by Chivers Press, England, and by G.K. Hall & Co., USA.

Published in 2000 in the U.K. by arrangement with the author c/o Golden West Literary Agency.

Published in 2000 in the U.S. by arrangement with Golden West Literary Agency.

U.K. Hardcover   ISBN 0-7540-4214-6   (Chivers Large Print)
U.K. Softcover   ISBN 0-7540-4215-4   (Camden Large Print)
U.S. Softcover   ISBN 0-7838-9091-5   (Nightingale Series Edition)

The text of this Large Print edition is unabridged.
Other aspects of the book may vary from the original edition.

Set in 16 pt. New Times Roman.

Printed in Great Britain on acid-free paper.

British Library Cataloguing in Publication Data available

Library of Congress Cataloging-in-Publication Data

Dean, Dudley.
    Trail of the hunter / Dudley Dean.
        p. cm.
    ISBN 0-7838-9091-5 (lg. print : sc : alk. paper)
    1. Large type books.   I. Title.
PS3554.E155 T7 2000
813'.54—dc21   00–039530

CHAPTER ONE

Justin Emery picked his brother up from the bloodied Texas dust and braced him against the front of the house that their father, Major Bert Emery, had built back in '66.

'Ford, you're the only man who could do this to me and live,' Justin said, breathing hard.

Ford Emery sagged against Justin's supporting fist clenched at the front of his shirt. Ford tried to breathe through his broken nose. He was twenty-two, five years younger than Justin. A deep cut above Ford's right eye bled across the cold November dust that caked his face.

'A lot of things you've done,' Justin said harshly, 'were excused by some because you were a kid. And other things you did later were excused because you were drunk.'

'Listen to me, Justin—'

'But you're no longer a kid. And today you're cold sober when you try to steal my wife!' Justin stepped back, flexing the fingers of his large hands. He was a strongly built man, black-haired, with a look of power about him.

Ford managed to stand erect for a moment without Justin to hold him; then his legs started to fold. He sprawled across the remains

1

of Samantha's garden, already killed by the icy winds sweeping down from the Panhandle and now thoroughly trampled during the fight.

During the savage encounter Samantha had stayed on the veranda, holding her torn yellow dress. Many times she had cried out to them to stop fighting. It was a waste of breath.

'Justin,' she pleaded, 'listen to what I have to say. Ford didn't try to steal me. You don't understand.'

'Understand?' Justin lifted his gaze to the handsome woman he had married, pale now under her rich yellow hair. 'I understand what my eyes can see.'

This morning he had been out to the south pasture, where he had dismounted to mend a break in the fence. His horse, spooked by something in the brush, attempted to jump the fence. It got hung up midway, with the barbs sawing at its belly. Before Justin could free it with wire cutters, the animal's frantic thrashing had cut it deeply. Justin was forced to shoot it.

He was making the two-mile walk back to the house, head down, cursing the wire that had destroyed his horse—the wire so necessary to a Texas spread the size of Hayfork. It was then that he saw Ford and Samantha behind the barn, Samantha's dress torn and Ford's hand slipped through the tear, cupping the white flesh of a breast.

Ten of the eighteen ranch hands here at the home place had ridden in during the battle.

2

They watched in awkward silence as the Emery boys slugged each other back and forth across the yard of this Hayfork ranch near Midpoint, Texas. This place and another Hayfork ranch in the Dakotas had been left to both sons by the late Major Emery. Even a man with half a brain could tell that after today things would never be the same between the brothers.

It was plain that Justin was losing no time in making a change. He dug a silver dollar from his pocket.

'Ford, you call it. Whichever you want, this place or the Ketcher place in Dakota. Whoever wins Ketcher gets a thousand head of beef from here to even things up.'

'Whatever you want,' Ford muttered through his broken mouth. 'I'll take heads.'

Justin flipped the coin. It made a silvery pattern as it caught feeble sunlight, then struck the ground. It rolled and came up heads.

'Your luck held,' Justin said, examining the silver dollar. 'Make your choice.'

'If there has to be a choice, I'll take this place.'

Justin picked up the coin, looked around at Ford lying in the flower garden below the veranda. Ford had the dark brown hair and eyes of their Georgia mother.

'Agreed,' Justin said. 'You now own the Midpoint place.'

Justin strode across the yard to where the

3

men stood, some with hands shoved into hip pockets. He addressed his foreman, Darsie Polk.

'Darsie, I'm taking a thousand head of beef to the Ketcher place. I want you to take the boys and round them up.'

Darsie Polk, who had ramrodded the Hayfork properties since the brand was established before the war, stared grimly across the yard at Samantha Emery on the veranda. He spat on a tuft of withered buffalo grass, then drew Justin away from the other hands. He was a stringy man with a squinting eye and a bad shoulder. Each week he trimmed his graying beard with a sharp knife.

'You hadn't oughta break up with Ford this way,' the foreman advised in his slow drawl.

'It's high time my brother learned there are some things in this world you don't excuse.'

Again Darsie Polk flicked a glance at Samantha, who stood tall, golden-haired, gripping the veranda rail. She stared down at Ford, but made no move to go to him. Ford was trying to get up.

'Having a pretty woman around a ranch,' Darsie Polk said, 'is 'most the same as a man trying to pound nails with the butt of a hair-trigger shotgun. Either way he's goin' to end up bloody.'

Justin's rage had spent itself, but he still felt thick with disgust and bitterness at what this day had brought.

4

'Darsie, you can also make a choice. You can stay with Ford—'

'I helped talk the Major into startin' the Ketcher place, so I feel sorta responsible for it.' The foreman spat again. 'Besides, you and me work good together. Ford—well, he ain't you, that's for sure.'

'I'm glad you'll be with me, Darsie.'

'There's only one thing. It's late November. It ain't a time to drive cows north.'

Justin glanced at the slate-blue sky. 'With any luck the weather will hold. We'll be at the Ketcher place the first week in January.'

'We might get hit by a blizzard.'

'Even blizzards don't last forever,' Justin said.

'Four months wouldn't be too long to wait. Then it'll be spring.'

'Four hours is really too long to wait. Start rounding up those cows, Darsie. I'll be out to give you a hand in a minute.'

Justin started for the house. He did not look at his wife as he climbed the veranda steps.

Darsie Polk turned to his segundo, Orion 'Smitty' Smith. Smitty was the only married ranch hand at this Midpoint place. He lived with his wife in a small house a mile from headquarters at Buffalo Creek.

'Smitty,' Darsie Polk said softly, 'trouble come to us on a high hoss the day Justin married the Widow Quine.'

CHAPTER TWO

Justin limped on a swelling ankle through the big parlor filled with furniture that the Major had freighted up from the Bend place when they had settled here right after the war. A daguerrotype of his mother on the wall above her New Orleans sofa caught his eye. She was a smiling woman who looked very much like Ford. He felt sick when he thought of her gentleness, her strength, and contrasted it to her son's weakness. Today Ford had completed his worthless cycle.

The tendons in Justin's neck swelled when his mind saw again the picture of Ford's brown hand against the curving mound of Samantha's breast.

Angrily he stalked into the large kitchen and splashed coffee into a tin cup, then laced it from a stone jug of Colonel's Choice. The jug of whisky he removed from its hiding place behind a stack of tinned goods. The jug was always kept out of view so as to lessen temptation for Ford when he came up to eat with them. Temptation! Justin set his teeth against the pain of his thoughts. He had kept a jug of whisky hidden from Ford. But he had neglected to hide his wife.

Tiredly he sank into a chair at the big kitchen table. He sipped from the cup, wrinkling his face at the strong whisky. He heard the rustle of Samantha's skirts, felt her nearness.

'Justin, the last thing in the world I wanted,' she whispered brokenly, 'was trouble between you and Ford.'

He drained his cup. The Colonel's Choice eased some of his tiredness. He twisted in his chair to look at her. Her full lips were bloodless, the wide blue eyes that he had found so fetching last year at the cattle association convention were now deeply troubled. In the lobby of the Empire Hotel, St. Louis, she had been the center of all eyes, and Justin knew she was the most stunning woman he had ever seen in his life. Sight of her had momentarily strangled his desire for power, his vow not to marry until he was thirty; the brilliance of her smile overshadowed his goal.

It had once been his hope that upon his thirtieth birthday he could sit in a luxurious leather chair in the lobby of the Bank of Chicago, smoke a dollar cigar, and be told that Hayfork properties, land, and cattle, were worth one million dollars.

Then in St. Louis last year he had considered himself the most fortunate of men when she agreed to marry him. When he brought her home to the Midpoint place, he worked harder than ever, driving himself toward the mark he had set for his thirtieth birthday, three years away. It was considerably out of reach, now that he had broken with Ford.

'If I hadn't come by when I did,' he said gruffly, 'what then? Inside the barn instead of out?'

'Justin, please—'

'In a pile of hay with your dress off?'

'No, Justin.' She was struggling to retain her poise. 'I needed someone to talk to.'

'Do you usually talk to a man with your bosom bared to his hand?'

'Ford lost his head, Justin. Can't you understand? He's young—he thinks he's in love with me.'

Justin took a deep breath, felt an ache in his side and wondered if Ford's fists had cracked a rib.

'Ford usually buys his pleasures at the Rainbow,' Justin said thinly. 'Of course that's foolish now, with my wife so close at hand.'

Samantha straightened there beside the table. 'Justin, you've said some cruel things to me. I've taken them because I love you.'

'You said you needed someone to talk to. Why Ford? Why not me?'

'With you out on the range at all hours? And you forbidding me to ride a horse or drive a wagon alone?'

'You know the reason for my concern,' he said, frowning.

'Yes, because of what happened to that girl so long ago.' Samantha lifted a hand. Sunlight touched her pink nails. 'When you do come home, all you talk is cattle. You never want to listen to what I have to say.'

'It's the first time I knew you were unhappy.'

She made a small gesture. 'Justin, it isn't unhappiness. You are my life.' She lowered her blue eyes. 'My other life—before I met you—was shadowed and filled with bitter memories.'

'I never asked you about your past.'

A faint smile strained the corners of her lovely mouth. 'You speak of my past as if it might be sinful.'

Pushing his cup aside, he looked around the big room with its huge stone fireplace, the rusted pothooks nowadays seldom used for cooking. Last year he had bought a Regers & Hare range for her. He stared at the scrubbed board floor, the curtains she had made for the windows. There was a woman's touch here, something they'd never had after their mother died, years back. Their father had returned from the war, a major out of Hood's brigade. He had taken up land here in '66, when stampeding buffalo would sometimes spread across the flats as far as a man could see. In twenty years the buffalo were gone. The land was shaping up, was civilized, almost. Now he was going to leave it, start his life anew up at the Ketcher place.

Samantha sank into a chair across the table from him. 'I love you deeply. But I'll go back to St. Louis if it will help patch up things between you and Ford.'

'You're staying with me.' He rose and tossed his cup into the dishpan. He looked around at her. Samantha's beauty never failed to stir him, especially when her full lips shaped themselves into that pensive, quizzical smile that was so much a part of her.

'What I'm wondering is this,' he said. 'When I was in Austin this spring and you were here alone with Ford—'

Her mouth paled. 'Is that what you think of me? That when your back is turned, I would go to your brother?'

'You must have done something to make Ford think he could—'

'Justin, you have a chance now to be rid of me. Haven't you noticed before this that wherever I go there's trouble?'

This he could not deny. It bothered him. And as Darsie Polk had pointed out once, 'It'll lead to a killing.'

Wherever he went men would turn to stare at Samantha. A hundred times he had tried to decide what it was that put the crazy heat in their eyes and made them reckless to the point of insanity. He'd fought with his fists over her half a dozen times during their courtship. Even before their marriage he had shot a cattle buyer in the leg when the man carried his ardor for Samantha too far and drew a derringer on Justin. It had happened in the

10

crowded lobby of the Empire Hotel. But since coming to Midpoint there had been no problems. Until today.

It was in her walk, he supposed, or the proud way she carried her head. He really didn't know just what it was.

'I'll ask you once,' Justin said. 'I hope you won't lie.'

'There was never anything between Ford and me.'

'Did you entice him, lead him on in any way?'

'Justin, I tried to be nice to him because he is your brother. We've had some talks about that girl you intended to marry, Elsie Gorman. We've talked of other things.' She got up from the table, one hand holding the torn bodice of her dress. 'Until today, he never put a hand on me.'

'I'd like to believe that.' Some of Justin's anger dissolved.

Samantha watched him, frowning. Today her yellow hair hung in two plaits down her back, nearly reaching her waist. 'We might as well go the rest of the way,' she plunged on, 'and bring up the matter I wanted to talk over with Ford.'

Mention of his brother's name sent Justin's gaze darting to the breast that pushed against the rip in the dress. 'I never want anything to remind me of this day. Not for as long as I live. Whatever it is you wanted to discuss with Ford

11

can wait.'

'Justin—'

'It can wait until we reach the Ketcher place. There we are going to pretend we're starting a new life together. As if we'd just been married. I don't want to remember this day.' He had been speaking louder than he intended. Now his voice tightened. 'Because on this day I came within a whisper of shooting my own brother.'

'Every time you look at me you'll be reminded of what happened. I would go away, if that would bring you and Ford back together.'

'Any brotherly feeling I had for Ford died in me years ago. He's done nothing since to win my respect. I've put up with him because he's my brother. After today he stands alone.'

'Justin, don't do this to him. Without you, he—'

Justin limped to the door on his bad ankle. He looked around. 'I'm going to town. Dobbs has to draw up papers that will split the ranches.'

'I'm asking you again, Justin, to sit down with me and—'

But he was gone. Soon she saw him ride toward the town of Midpoint on a paint horse, a big man hunched in the saddle, his face skinned from his brother's fists.

Slowly Samantha turned to stare at the mound of ashes in the stone fireplace at the far end of the room. Some of the ashes were from the letter that had arrived here for her last week. Justin had brought the mail out from Midpoint, but he had shown no interest in the letter with the St. Louis postmark. He put all his attention on a copy of the *Stockman's Journal* that had arrived in the same mail.

The letter was from Samantha's old friend Mary Hope. Closing her eyes, Samantha could visualize the words that had put a burgeoning terror in her breast:

'Just a hurried note to warn you that a man claiming to be your husband is making inquiries here . . .'

For two days Samantha had pondered the problem of bringing the matter to Justin's attention. On two occasions she tried to get him to listen to her, but he seemed preoccupied with business problems. The rainless spring and summer of '85 had pushed the less stable outfits into bankruptcy. Justin had borrowed heavily on the Ketcher place to keep them going until beef could be sold in the spring. This morning she had made her decision. She would ask Ford's advice.

But things had turned out differently.

She stood alone in the big kitchen of the quiet house where she had come as Justin's bride. Now she tried to view her problem objectively. Mary Hope must have misunderstood, been overly concerned for an

13

old friend.

There was no reason to suppose that Erdman Quine was once again walking this earth a free man.

Back in St. Louis, she had lied to Justin. It was her only deceit. Today she had started to pay the price—for Justin had broken with his brother.

CHAPTER THREE

As he rode toward town, Justin considered his position.

Both Hayfork ranches were prosperous, even though the Ketcher place was heavily in debt. After the cattlemen's association convention in St. Louis last year the business had seemed more stable than ever before. There was talk of a national cattle trail from Texas to the northern ranges. And the cattlemen, solidly organized at last, were thumbing their noses at the railroads, because it was cheaper to drive cattle than to ship them. It looked as if there would be great years ahead.

But the fight with Ford today and the resultant splitting of the ranches would mean a readjustment in Justin's long-range plans.

Once at the Ketcher place, he would get his roots down solidly. He could still borrow more on the ranch; he'd take a look at Wyoming and Montana, spread his fences. Achieving his goal might have to be postponed; it would take more than three years now. But he'd make it, damn if he wouldn't.

*   *   *

Midpoint, Texas, reflected the general prosperity of the ranching business. Two buildings of cut stone were rising in the mercantile block, and these days you saw matched teams and fancy buggies; ranchers' wives in brocade and silk instead of patched calico.

In the office above the Great Western Feed Company, Justin explained to Edgar Dobbs the kind of legal documents he wanted drawn up. Dobbs, a fat man who had prospered more in cattle than in law, tried to argue Justin out of it. He had been a great friend of the late Major Bert Emery. Last year Dobbs had sold off a herd of beef and a few sections of land east of town to Chicagoans for $340,000. His wife and daughters were now in Europe enjoying the proceeds of that deal.

'It isn't right for you to do this,' Dobbs said, when he had finished writing out the agreements and had made copies in the letterpress. 'The Major wanted you and Ford to share everything equal.' Dobbs' careless chewing of tobacco resulted in stains on the

15

expensive suits bought for him by his wife.

'The Midpoint place is Ford's responsibility now,' Justin said.

'What finally broke you two up?' Dobbs asked. 'Was it that old trouble?'

Justin stood at a window overlooking the street, where he could see a bull team hauling in a wagonload of buffalo bones from the flats south of town.

'Edgar, I don't want to talk about it.'

Dobbs cleared his throat, his eyes thoughtful in his round wind-burned face. He got up and came and stood beside Justin. 'I've known you since you were head high to a newborn calf. I had a drink with the Major on the day your brother was born. So I feel I have a right to speak. You shouldn't hold it against Ford for what happened to Elsie. It was years back, and time heals everything.'

'Hardly,' Justin said.

'If it wasn't that old trouble that broke you and Ford up, it must've been something your wife did—'

'Kindly leave Samantha out of this discussion.'

Justin glared. On Dobbs' left hand a diamond ring reflected sunlight. It was his only personal extravagance. Justin knew he had paid ten thousand dollars for it in New York last year. Thoughtfully Dobbs rubbed the diamond across his vest that was spotted with tobacco stains.

16

'You can beat hell out of me if you want, Justin, but I aim to have my say. That girl you married—I like her.' Dobbs hurried on when Justin started to protest angrily. 'But there's something about her that puts a man on edge. I swear, when you bring her to town you can almost feel the tension in every man present.'

Justin shoved into the pocket of his leather coat the agreements the lawyer had drawn up. 'When I married Mrs Quine,' Justine said quietly, 'the preacher made it plain it was till death do us part. That's how it stays, Edgar.'

'I wasn't aiming to try and split you.'

'What do I owe you for drawing up these papers?'

'Justin, I was only trying to point out that I can see how a young fella Ford's age might go kind of loco around a woman like Samantha.'

'I see somebody has beat me to town with the whole story,' Justin said thinly.

'You know how news travels in this country. One of your hands brought it in.'

Justin stepped to the door: There he paused a moment, hating to leave with bitterness between them. 'Edgar, if you ever get up north to Ketcher, you look us up, you hear?'

'You could lose a lot of money making a drive this time of year. You ever think of that?'

'There's three thousand head of beef at the Ketcher place,' Justin said. 'If I lose half the thousand head I drive north I'll still be in good shape.'

17

'I declare, you got the Major's mule blood in you for sure.'

They shook hands silently; then Justin's bootheels clattered on the outside stairway.

*　　*　　*

In Teakant's Rainbow Saloon, Justin was met by the steamy odor of damp wool and whisky. Men who had been crowded around the big stove in the overheated room came to stand with Justin at the bar.

A very thin, stooped rancher named Cob Shandy, wearing an expensive Denver suit, touched Justin's arm. 'Hear you're pullin' out. All I can say is I hope the drought don't reach clear up to the Ketcher place.' If Texas didn't get rain by next spring, Shandy predicted dolefully, the golden cattle market might very well start to sag.

Lew Teakant came down the bar, rubbing a hand over his bald head. 'Sure hate to lose you, Justin,' he said earnestly. The saloonman chewed an unlighted cigar. From the rooms above the saloon came a girl's sudden high-pitched laughter. Teakant went on, 'Specially hate to think that good-looking wife of yours won't be around town no more.' He smiled, trying to make a joke of it.

Cob Shandy said, 'I tell you, seein' Samantha Emery in town is like bringin' the first warm sun of spring to Midpoint.'

Another man spoke up. 'Why, I know boys at the RB spread that'll ride in thirty miles on the Saturday they know you'll bring her to town when you come in to do your buying.'

'Brings comfort to a lonely man to see a woman like that,' said Shandy.

'A well-set-up woman she is,' reflected Lew Teakant. And he instantly paled when Justin's cold gray eyes fell upon him. 'Justin, it was meant as a compliment.'

Justin placed a gold piece on the bar. 'Lew, I'm buying the boys a final drink. And have one yourself.'

There was a clearing of throats. Teakant set out a bottle of Colonel's Choice. Glasses were raised.

'We wish you luck, Justin,' they said.

'Maybe I'll see some of you boys in Chicago, come shipping time,' Justin said. 'I hope so.'

After Justin had shaken hands all around, Lew Teakant followed him outside. 'We're goin' to miss you, Justin. Damn if we ain't. Hayfork at Midpoint won't be much without you to run it.'

'The Major left Ford a big pair of boots to fill.' Justin's voice hardened. 'Reckon it's high time he made a move to fill 'em.'

Teakant shifted his cigar, looking doleful. 'We hear you and Ford fought over your wife.'

'I don't wish to discuss it.' Justin swung into the saddle.

'I didn't mean it personal. Only—Well, I

19

dunno why, but a man seems to feel different when he knows a woman's had more'n one husband.'

'We're friends now, Lew,' Justin said from the saddle. 'Let's part that way.'

'I only meant she's a fine lady, but bein' a widow woman, maybe Ford—'

Justin rode away. A hundred yards beyond the last building at Midpoint, Justin turned in the saddle, his heart squeezing into a hard knot under his breastbone. He thought of the years he had ridden this road; in summer heat and dust and in the winter when blue northers punished man and horse.

Here in Midpoint he'd had his first love, Elsie Gorman. When she died tragically he vowed he would not marry until thirty, if at all. Justin rubbed a hand along his side where the soreness caused by his brother's fists made breathing difficult.

He thought of his years with Ford. Going to the Midpoint school, they would leave two hours early and mend fence along the way. After school they would ride home by a different route and fix fence again. He and the Major and Ford could stretch a mile of fence in a day if they really bent their backs to it.

When they were younger it was Justin who defended Ford, using fists on those who sought to badger the younger Emery boy. Maybe that was part of Ford's trouble, Justin thought as he started riding for Hayfork again. Kids today

20

were too soft. Ford had never had to face up to things on his own.

First there had been the Major to make things easy for him. 'The boy has your mother's eyes. You're stronger, but I declare that boy twists something up inside me, because I see your mother's face in his.'

It used to rankle Justin on occasion; he knew the Major favored Ford.

Only once had the Major lost his temper with Ford. That day he had whipped him with a buggy whip until he bled.

As Justin rode away from the town he had known so long, he thought of the years when his father refused to do business with a Northerner, except through a third party. But in the last year of his life the Major had expressed a change of feeling when he and Justin were riding this same road out of Midpoint.

'Hard to realize it was two decades ago,' the Major said that day, 'that Darsie Polk and me were shooting at the blue bellies. And they were trying their damndest to kill us. All sort of hazy now. I find my hate grows thin, like my blood.'

A week later the Major took sick and called Justin to his bed. 'Boy, you work too hard. You haven't had many pleasures. I want you to take yourself a wife. Don't spend your life grieving over Elsie.'

'Elsie's so dim, Major, I find it hard to

remember her face.'

'A man never knows what it is to have the steady comfort of a woman under his roof. Sometimes I miss your mother so bad the ache in me is almost too much.'

'I know, Major, I know.'

'I've plumb wore myself out fightin' myself and the world. Mostly myself, I reckon.'

'Rest easy now, Major, hear?'

'Make it up to Ford, about Elsie.'

Staring down at this father he felt he sometimes hardly knew, this military man, Justin thought: If you hadn't taken in a pair of half-broken bay horses in a swap—horses which you intended to break fully and use as a wagon team of high steppers when you went to town—If you hadn't done that, Major my father, Elsie would still be alive.

Two days later Major Bertram Austin Emery was dead . . .

Justin entered the lean-to built onto a wall of the bunkhouse. It had been erected last year as bachelor quarters for Ford when Justin brought home his bride.

Ford lay on his bed, staring at the ceiling. Across the room, above a desk, was a shelf of books Ford had brought home from the new college out at a place called Berkeley in California. He had quit after one year.

'Ford, do you feel up to holding a pen?'

Ford turned his head. Justin, looking down at him, wondered whether he would recognize

22

his own brother if he met him on the street today. Ford's face was swollen, misshapen, the lips puffed and cut. Never again would the nose resume its original shape.

'Justin, why don't you take a gun and kill me?' Ford said. 'You've wanted to long enough.'

'Don't feel sorry for yourself.'

'Since my twelfth year, to be exact, you've wished me dead.'

Justin laid the papers on the desk. 'Here's the agreement. I give up all claim to the Midpoint place. You give up all claim to the holdings in Dakota. I take one thousand head of beef.'

'She could grow old living with you, Justin,' Ford said, pushing himself to an elbow. 'You have no love, no warmth in you.'

'Keep it shut, Ford.'

'I could give her something.'

'Give her something?' Justin's gaze was flat gray steel. 'You tore her dress trying to force yourself. There is a word for it.'

'I wasn't trying to force myself,' came the voice from the beaten face. 'I think too much of her for that. I lost my head; that I admit.'

'Have those papers signed and witnessed by the time I pull out,' Justin said, and swung toward the door.

* * *

23

During the following days Justin threw himself feverishly into the job of forming up a herd. The Hayfork men stationed at line shacks had heard the word that he was pulling out. They all wanted to go north with him. Regretfully Justin informed them he couldn't take the entire crew because he was already overloaded at the Ketcher place with sixteen men. Those he couldn't take north with him were welcome to stay and work for Ford. But those not going on the drive asked for their time. Justin did not try and urge them to stay. It was Ford's problem to get a crew to work for him.

All during the gather a vicious thought kept sliding into Justin's mind: How much of it was Ford's fault? How much of it Samantha's? Oh, it hadn't been a sudden thing. For months he had noticed the way Ford would watch her as if enraptured; the way Samantha would smile at him or touch his hand when he jumped forward to help her with a chair, or to open a door.

He remembered what Darsie Polk had asked one day: 'How'd she get to be a widow, anyhow?'

'Her husband died out in Arizona, and she came back to St. Louis. She'd lived there as a girl.'

'That all you know about her?'

'When you love a woman—in one blinding flash—there is nothing you need to know.'

At the time his foreman's question had

24

nettled him. Now Justin began to wonder if he really knew Samantha at all.

CHAPTER FOUR

Since the fight with Ford, Justin had slept on a horsehide sofa in the parlor. On the morning they were to pull out, he rose in the cold of dawn. Through the window he could see a few strips of ice fingering the shadowed places on the ground. He wondered if during the night the gather had strayed. The cows were hard to hold, having a tendency to turn their rumps to the wind and drift south.

Samantha appeared from the bedroom, plaits of pale hair pushing the front of a blue nightdress against her breasts. Justin's throat tightened as he stomped into his cold boots. Only a few pieces of furniture remained. The rest had already been loaded into a wagon.

'Justin, are we going to leave this place without love?' she asked, her voice troubled.

He looked around as she lifted a hand to him. Every movement of the lithe body seemed to call her to the attention of men— her delicate shift of shoulder or hand, her walk, the way she arched her brows. She had that rare gift of seeming to be impressed when a man spoke, watching him intently with large eyes, her lips parted in a soft smile. She had a way of touching her lips with the tip of her tongue. Her voice was deep for a woman, vibrant, yet gentle. He had realized long ago that her entry into a room was a delight to the senses of every man present.

'Make it easy on me, Samantha,' he said, clenching his teeth. 'Wait until we reach the Ketcher place.'

'Will the Ketcher place soften you toward me?'

'I hope it will,' he said. 'You'd better put on some clothes before you take cold.'

'I might as well. I can see my attire gives you no pleasure.'

Sounds of the men stirring in the bunkhouse reached them.

Samantha bit her lip, turned away, then looked back. 'Are we always going to be apart?'

'Give me time to think, to clear my head, will you?'

He strode to the cookshack where the men would be taking their last meal under a roof for some weeks.

Darsie Polk's breath was steaming when he came in from a wash at the pump. 'Justin, I done some fool things in my time,' the old man said. 'But for sure, I never figured to start a trail drive north on the first of December.' When Justin made no reply, Polk went on, 'You aim to say goodbye to your brother?'

'I intend to see him, yes.'

26

Justin found Ford in the lean-to. The papers had been signed. Ford's face was still swollen. Justin put his copies of the agreement into his pocket and sniffed the air.

'Surprised you haven't tried to hide in a vat of whisky,' Justin said.

'I stayed sober. Only because you'd expect me to get drunk. I won't give you that satisfaction.'

They eyed each other for a moment. 'Remember this,' Justin said, feeling a faint pity. 'If you ever need help real bad, I'm still your brother.'

'And you remember this. You be good to her!'

'A holy attitude for a man to take,' Justin said coldly, 'considering that he sneaks behind the barn with his brother's wife.'

Ford's cheeks were flushed. 'I didn't sneak.'

'Stay here in Texas,' Justin warned. 'Don't try and get in touch with her, ever.'

Ford just looked at him.

After a time Justin said awkwardly, 'Ford, let me give you some advice—'

'Advice is one thing you've always been free with. You can tell other people how to live their lives. Sometimes you've been a little careless with how you've lived your own.'

Justin swallowed, knowing Ford was throwing it up to him about the days that followed roundup. Or maybe coming home from a trail drive. The days when you slowly

27

let the taut wires out of your system, following the days on end, the hours in the saddle. The responsibility. The hundred and one problems that beset a rancher these days. You could go berserk and start shooting up a saloon, as had happened. You could gamble and lose it all over a game of cards. Or you could fight with your fists and find a woman and a jug of whisky and—

Justin said, 'I haven't done those things since I've been married.'

'Maybe you should tell Samantha what a heller you used to be.'

'I imagine she knows I've been no saint.'

Ford turned his head. 'She's a lady. I hope you always treat her like one.'

Justin's short laugh had the sound of a shard of glass scraped on metal. 'You're the one forgot to treat her like a lady.'

Justin walked out, slamming the door. As he started for the house where the men were loading the rest of the furniture into a wagon, Darsie Polk tried to match his long stride.

'You make it up with Ford at all?' the foreman asked.

'Ford didn't want it that way.' Justin felt the cold December air against his heated face. Damn the nerve of Ford, warning him about Samantha!

Darsie Polk rubbed his bearded chin. 'I ain't forgiving Ford, you understand. But sometimes a man has so much on his conscience it makes him do loco things.'

'Whatever you had on your conscience, Darsie, you'd face up to. You wouldn't become a drunken sneak like Ford.'

'There are times when facin' up ain't easy, Justin. You ever hear the smooth deadly sound of a Gatling gun?'

'No. But I remember the Major had a gun like that. I saw it once when I was a boy. In the barn, hidden under some hay.'

'Sometimes I wake up at night and see that gun and I have a powerful urge to scream. So you see, I know how Ford feels, mebby. He sees the dead face of Elsie Gorman. And I see—'

'Don't defend Ford, damn it, Darsie. Let him defend himself.'

That day they only made ten miles, with the cows not liking it. Justin wondered how many added miles he and the crew had ridden, shunting strays back into the herd.

But the following days found the cattle a little easier to drive.

CHAPTER FIVE

The three men arrived in Midpoint, Texas in mid-December, riding shaggy horses splattered with mud. There was little to call attention to them on this blustery day save

29

their urgency. One of the men was better dressed than his two companions. His intelligent hazel eyes were narrowed against the wind as he drew rein and thoughtfully studied the sign over Teakant's Rainbow Saloon.

The man to his right was outstandingly large, even in a country full of big men. Upon his face were the marks of old brawls. His right cheek was scarred as if the flesh had once been pierced by the point of a knife. His nose was flat. His face was raw from the cold.

The third man was black-haired, with slate-colored eyes in a long brown face.

The first man said, 'We'll try here,' and led the way into the saloon.

Only a dozen or so men lounged around the stove this day. They broke off their talk to study the strangers.

Teakant, settling his teeth in the butt of a soggy cigar, said, 'Your pleasure, gents?'

The hazel-eyed man studied him for a moment, then smiled. 'A little Colonel's Choice would be fine for me.' He turned. 'How about you, Charlie? And you, Kelso?'

Charlie Ivory swelled his large chest and said, 'Fine with me, Erd.'

Kelso Kane grunted and said, 'Whisky is whisky.' Kane was lithe, shorter than Erdman Quine, narrower through the shoulders.

Teakant removed a bottle from the backbar. 'You gents are in luck. It's the last Colonel's

30

Choice I have.'

Erd Quine seemed interested. He licked at the uneven line of a thick copper-colored mustache. He was tall, only an inch under six feet, but he was overshadowed by Charlie Ivory. At first glance he seemed slender, but with his fur-lined jacket thrown open to the room's heat there was no mistaking the power in neck and shoulders. The tip of his rather long nose was peeling, from snow glare probably. He looked to be in his early thirties.

Quine filled his glass and made a show of studying it against the light that filtered through the leaded glass of the doors. 'Fella in St. Louis drank this brand of whisky, so I hear.'

Teakant shrugged. 'Well, it costs a little more'n average. I used to buy it regular for Justin Emery. He was down to one bottle when he pulled out.'

Quine showed a mild surprise. 'Small world. Come to think of it, that fella in St. Louis was named Justin Emery.'

Teakant laid his cigar on the lip of the bar. 'Justin was in St. Louis, all right. Last year, for the cattle association convention.'

Kelso Kane rubbed a spot of mud off his chin. 'If Emery's pulled out,' he said in a flat voice, 'it looks like we had a long ride for nothing.'

'Ride wasn't wasted,' Quine said. He turned to Teakant. 'When did Emery leave here?'

'Few weeks back,' Teakant said.

31

'Where did he go?'

The saloonman started to reply; then his face closed. 'Don't make it a practice to discuss a man's business with strangers.'

Quine only smiled, but Kelso Kane's slate-colored eyes narrowed. 'You talk right up, for a little man, now don't you?' he said in a quiet but somehow deadly voice. He looked as if he might enjoy reaching across the bar to grab Teakant by the throat.

Teakant paled a little around the mouth. 'Any information you want,' he said stubbornly, 'about Justin Emery, you can get from his brother at Hayfork, eight miles west of town.'

'That's mighty kind of you, sir,' Quine drawled. He finished his drink and placed a coin beside the empty glass. 'Fine whisky. Justin Emery has good taste in more things than one.'

'We thought a lot of him,' Teakant said. 'We still do.'

'I shouldn't wonder,' Quine said, holding the saloonman's eye. 'But every thief has his dark side, if you look for it long enough.'

There was a stunned silence in the room as the trio headed for the doors, Quine in the lead. Charlie Ivory, swinging his long arms, turned to give the men around the stove a hard look. Kelso Kane was lacing up his blanket coat so it covered a revolver that rode low in a cut-down holster.

Teakant and the others watched them mount and ride past the steamed-up windows. It was unusual to find men out horsebacking the miles in such lonely country this time of year—unless they had an almighty important reason for so doing.

Teakant picked up his cigar, musing, 'The one with the mustache has the marks of a gentleman. But that damn smile of his chills the blood.'

'Them other two struck me as gunslingers,' said the red-haired Cob Shandy.

'Hope Ford don't get the fool notion of hiring on men like that,' said Solly Granger of the Midpoint Livery. 'Ford can use men, all right, seein' as how his crew quit on him, but—'

'Funny thing about those three fellas wanting Justin,' Edgar Dobbs said, frowning. He turned from the stove, where he had been warming his plump hands. 'Sort of worries me.'

'I recollect them kind in Abilene back in sixty-seven or thereabouts,' said Cob Shandy. 'Something about the eyes.'

'We ain't had a killin' around here in three months or more,' said Teakant. 'Country's growin' up. Looks like the old days are gone for good.'

Edgar Dobbs was staring toward the street. 'When I see a trio like that,' the lawyer observed, 'I begin to wonder if the old days are really gone.'

'Cattle business is also growin' up,' said Lew

Teakant. 'I'm goin' to miss Justin around here, damn it.'

'And miss watching that wife of his when she comes to town,' said Solly Granger.

Teakant set out bottles for some of the men. 'That woman will likely get a man killed one day. I said that the first time I laid eyes on her.'

'There's something about her, damn if there ain't,' Cob Shandy said, bending his lank frame at the bar. 'She walks along the street and the first thing a man thinks about is beddin' down.'

Teakant helped himself to a drink. 'It's the way she walks, I reckon,' he mused. 'She lifts her arm, even, and it turns a man's blood hot.'

'My old woman lifts her arm,' said one of the men, with a laugh, 'and it does not one damn thing to me.'

'Sometimes I feel right sorry for Justin,' Teakant said. He finished his drink. 'He figured to marry with Elsie Gorman when he turned nineteen. They'd been married for years now, had she lived.'

'Justin's never forgot it was on account of Ford that Elsie got killed,' said Cob Shandy.

Solly Granger said, 'I hear Justin ain't been out to Elsie's grave since he married.'

'He's likely got Elsie out of his system,' said Teakant. 'But he'll never forgive Ford.'

'Too bad,' said Granger, 'that when Justin finally did marry, he got a woman who gives a man crotch-ache every time he sees her.

34

Remember that kid Ben I had working for me last summer? Well, she smiled at Ben one day when he was forkin' hay. You know that sorta smile she's got.'

'Yeah,' Edgar Dobbs observed. 'Stiffens the short hairs at the back of your neck.'

'Ain't all it does to a man,' said Cob Shandy.

Solly Granger leaned plump forearms on the bar and grew confidential. 'Well, Ben got the idea she was in love with him. Just 'cause she smiled. Next time she come to town Ben tried to pin her in a corner. I fired him right then and there. I said if he wasn't gone from the country by sundown I'd have to tell Justin.'

'God knows what Justin would've done to him,' Teakant said.

'Ben got outa town like he was ridin' a jag of lightning,' Solly Granger said.

'So that's what happened to Ben,' Teakant cut in. 'Never did hear why he got out so sudden.'

'Major Emery made fortunes and he lost 'em,' Teakant observed. 'He wanted those two boys of his to run things equal. Too bad the woman come between 'em.'

'If it wasn't the woman it'd have been something else,' Cob Shandy said, tipping his hat back on his red head. 'Justin's never had any love for Ford—on account of Ford the same as put a gun to the head of Elsie Gorman and pulled the trigger.'

'Ford was only twelve years old at the time,'

35

defended Edgar Dobbs. 'Just a boy.'

'Boy!' exclaimed Teakant. 'Maybe a boy these days, 'cause the kids are softer than they was in my time. Talk about boys—let me tell you something. My older brother packed me on his back all the way from Monterrey, Mexico, when our folks was killed there. Clear to San Antone, with his bare feet bleedin'. He was ten years old. Don't talk to me about a boy twelve not bein' a man. In Texas he damn well better be a man or he won't live to see twenty.' Then Teakant's face changed. 'At least it was so in them days.'

'Times are different,' said Edgar Dobbs and, without taking aim, fired expertly at a cuspidor near his feet. 'But I do predict Ford won't last the year at Hayfork. He'll lose the Midpoint place to the bank, sure as hell.'

CHAPTER SIX

During Ford's drunk, while he was alone at the Midpoint place after Justin pulled out, Elsie Gorman appeared in his nightmares. He could see her small vibrant face, the dark eyes and the black hair. At times he could see her clearly, holding out a very pale hand to him and saying, 'Ford, it was not your fault.'

And at other times her eyes would accuse him and she would say in a sad voice, 'Why did you do it, Ford? Why did you do it to me?'

She was four years older than Ford and he had thought he was in love with her. Whenever she came over with her folks for Sunday dinner, Ford would climb the barn roof, hoping that she witnessed his daring. Sometimes he would walk the top rail of the corral fence.

When he was ten he rode a half-broken horse for her approval and he was thrown. His broken arm had to be set by Doc Winters in Midpoint.

The Major said. 'You'll break your fool neck one day, showing off in front of a pretty girl.'

Later, when he was twelve, Elsie would give him an indulgent smile, when he resumed what he considered to be acts of bravery.

Forcibly he terminated the nightmares by breaking the last jug of whisky. He threw it out into the yard, adding to the collection of other jugs.

He heated water and shaved, feeling utterly alone. His hand shook so that his face, still bruised from his encounter with Justin, was badly nicked.

He forced himself to think of the present. Samantha was of the present. Elsie Gorman was in the past, the dead past.

On this day he was hunched on his bed, holding Samantha's glove—all he had to remind him that she lived and breathed the same earth's air. He pressed the soft leather to

37

his cheek, aware of a faint scent of lilac that stirred him deeply. He closed his eyes, letting her drift back into his consciousness. He remembered her softness that day by the barn. Memory of that moment was torn with confusion.

The morning of the incident she had whispered, 'Ford, dear, will you meet me by the barn?' She seemed worried, and had pressed his hand with her warm fingers. 'I have something to tell you, Ford,' she continued, those large eyes so intent on his face that he felt a sudden wash of heat through his whole body.

'I'll be there any time you want,' he had said hoarsely.

'In an hour. Justin will be gone by then, I'm sure.'

Meet me at the barn . . . Justin will be gone by then, I'm sure . . . I have something to tell you, Ford . . . Ford, dear . . .

And then finding her there by the weathered planks of the barn wall. So appealing, her beautiful face troubled. His hands went out to her, his embrace so sudden that she gave a small cry of pain or surprise.

Then Justin's voice harsh in his ear: 'I knew if I gave you enough rope—' Justin's fist smashing him in the face—

Now the sound of horses in the yard alerted him. He knew he had to stir; to forget Samantha, or try to. He had a crew to hire, a ranch to run.

Dropping the glove into a drawer, he stepped outside. He lifted a hand to shield his eyes against the reflection of sun against a paper-thin sheet of ice across the yard. He saw that three men had drawn rein some dozen feet away. They were muddied, their horses steaming against the cold.

When they just stared at him, Ford said, 'Did they send you out from town?'

'In a way,' said the one with the copper-colored mustache. 'You're the brother.'

'I'm Ford Emery. I need riders.' His voice was still thick from trying to drink dry this end of Texas. 'I also need a cook and a wrangler.' Then Ford realized these men had not come out to hire on. There was something about the way they looked at him that put a chill along his spine.

Ford shifted his gaze. The big one in the saddle looked as if he made brawling his life. The other man was lank, with a long brown face, wearing a blanket coat, the tail of which was pushed back beyond the walnut grips of a revolver.

'So your brother took your crew when he pulled out,' said the one with the mustache, looking around. He drew off his gloves. His clothing seemed fairly new. He dismounted. 'What happened to your face?'

'I was in a fight some weeks back. If it's any of your business.' Ford steadied his bloodshot eyes. 'Just who are you, anyway?'

'Erdman Quine is the name.' He saw the surprise on Ford's face, then said, 'I see it means something to you.'

Ford shook his head, trying to think clearly, but his mind was dulled by a black fog of alcohol. 'Her name was Quine once. Samantha Quine.'

'Her name is still Samantha Quine.'

Ford felt a flutter of fear in his stomach. The man was quite handsome, he decided. Winter sun touched the ends of thick copper hair that curled from under his hat. Ford looked around at the lean-to, wondering why he had been fool enough to leave his gun.

'You're an imposter,' said Ford, facing the riders again. 'Samantha's former husband is dead. Buried out in Arizona.'

'Buried out in Arizona for a time, yes,' Quine said. 'And while my back was turned she started living with your brother.'

Ford started backing toward the lean-to, the unhealed places on his face now livid. 'I won't stand for you insulting her!'

'How can you insult the kind of woman who'd desert her husband and run off with another man?'

Ford made a sweeping gesture with a hand that shook. 'Get off my property!'

'Where did your brother take my wife?' Quine demanded, his face hard.

'*Your* wife!'

40

'I married Samantha some years ago in Tucson.'

With a cry of frustration and rage, Ford darted for the lean-to. Kelso Kane almost lazily drew his revolver and fired. Splinters flew and the lean-to door trembled under the impact of the bullet. Ford froze.

'One more step,' Kane drawled, 'and your brains will be on the ground.'

Slowly Ford turned, staring at the gun in Kane's hand. His knees were shaking. 'All of you clear out,' Ford ordered, and felt a flush of humiliation because his voice had cracked under stress.

Quine laughed. 'Bet you're in love with her.'

'What if I am?' Ford felt a torn place on the right side of his shirt; the bullet had come that close to him.

'I'm also guessing that's why your face is marked up. Samantha always brings out the worst in a man.' Quine leaned forward. 'Where did they go?'

Ford shook his head. 'You're not going to get one damn thing out of me, and I mean it!'

'I can ride back to town and probably wheedle the information out of somebody. But it would be a waste of time as long as you're here to tell me.' Quine said something under his breath to his companions.

The two men dismounted and began snaking in from two sides. Ford felt a quiver of fear move from his stomach up into his throat.

'Charlie,' Quine said to the big man, 'you remember how you cut the bull calves in the spring?'

'I remember.' Charlie Ivory smiled. He drew a long-bladed knife from under his fleece-lined coat.

Quine laughed at the sudden terror in Ford's eyes. 'Don't look so surprised. You should be able to figure what Charlie is going to do. You've probably cut your own share of bull calves.'

Desperately, Ford again tried to reach the door of the lean-to—the door that now bore a fresh bullethole. His gun was just inside, on the desk.

But before he could reach the door Ivory and Kane grabbed him by the arms. They twisted him around so his back was to the lean-to. Quine came in suddenly and lashed out with a forearm at Ford's throat, jamming his head back against the door.

Quine said coldly, 'Cut his pants loose, Charlie, and show him how it's done.'

'Oh, Jeezus, no!' Ford screamed, as the knife blade began to saw into his belt. 'I'll tell you what you want to know.'

'Where did your brother take my wife?'

Ford gasped, trying to speak. The knife sawed deeper.

'North to Dakota,' he managed to say. 'Twenty miles from a town called Ketcher. We own—I mean, Justin owns a ranch there.

Don't—don't—for God's sake don't use the knife.'

'Dakota's a big place,' Quine mused. 'How is your brother traveling?'

'He took a herd north. They'll leave a wide trail.'

'Trailing cattle this time of year?'

'Justin thinks he can do anything,' Ford said, breathing hard. Despite his fear, bitterness crept into his voice.

Without warning, Quine struck him savagely on the jaw. Ford's knees caved and he fell against the cold ground.

Presently Ivory came tramping out of the lean-to. He carried Ford's rifle and revolver. 'It's all I could find around the place, Erd,' the big man said. 'Everything's cleaned out.'

Quine looked down at Ford. 'Emery, if you've got a gun around here Charlie didn't find, don't try and use it. You can't get all three of us.' Then, to emphasize the warning, he kicked Ford in the ribs.

For some minutes Ford tried to get back the breath Quine's boot toe had driven out of him. Finally he was able to stagger into the lean-to. Although he searched frantically, all he found was a derringer with a broken spring.

Even the empty bunkhouse revealed no weapon, and why should it? None of the hands would be foolish enough to leave behind when they quit a gun that was in working order.

When again he came outside to scan the

43

cold horizon, there was no sign of the three men. He began to calm, to organize his thoughts; the whisky and the fear and the beating had shaken him.

Then a wash of guilt swept over him. What of his own actions this day? He shuddered. How did you separate valor from common sense? Instinct told him that the big man would have used the knife on him had he refused to talk. They were that sort, all of them. But though he tried to justify his own actions, he could not escape a measure of self-contempt. Even though the knife had not been used he still felt like half a man.

He stood under the pale sun, thinking of Quine and Samantha. What could have possessed such a gentle girl to marry a man like Quine? And why was this Quine alive and not dead? Providing he was not lying.

Samantha would have an explanation, of course. But in the meantime, she would be in danger from such a man. And so would Justin, for that matter, Ford decided, feeling a tug of loyalty.

As he stood under the feeble sun he tried to decide what to do. Even though he'd made a dozen trips from this ranch to the Ketcher place in Dakota, he really had not been touched by life. Oh, he had observed rough men in some of the saloons and way-stations along the trail. He had seen men beaten, and one man shot in a brawl in Kansas. But so far he had been only an observer.

Sweat broke coldly along his back when be thought of perhaps meeting up with the trio again. How could he get word to Justin? He could ride to the railroad and use the telegraph. But there were no wires at Ketcher. How did you telegraph a trail herd somewhere in Kansas, perhaps along the Colorado border, maybe even now in Nebraska?

Dressing in his warmest clothing, Ford rode to Midpoint. When he tried the door of the hardware store and found it locked, he realized today was Sunday. Then he crossed to Teakant's Rainbow. Just as he reached the walk a thin-faced girl tapped on an upstairs window with her ring.

He looked up and saw her lips form a silent greeting, 'Hello Ford, honey.'

He gave her an absent wave of the hand and entered the saloon, his face set. 'Lew,' he said to Teakant, 'I need a rifle and a revolver and some shells. I know you have a few you've collected for whisky bills. I'll pay you when I come back from the Ketcher place.'

Teakant squinted at him. 'I got a hunch it has something to do with them three fellas who were asking about Justin.'

'You'll do me a favor,' Ford said stiffly, 'if you don't ask questions.'

Frowning, Teakant opened a closet door at the end of the bar. While the other patrons looked on silently, Ford selected a Winchester

75, a .44 revolver, and shells for each. Although the weapons were not new, they were the best of the lot.

Ford strode out, the rifle under his arm, the revolver in his belt.

He heard someone say, 'And he never even asked for a glass of whisky.'

The doors swung closed behind him. Ford stood for a moment on the walk, feeling the cold against his face; he heard again the rapping on the upstairs window.

An incipient loneliness began to seep through him. Upstairs he could forget. Up there were the only kind of girls he had ever sought out. For they were the sort who did not ask questions of a man, who did not pry and probe and one day look upon him with loathing and say, 'My God, you the same as murdered your brother's betrothed.'

Except for visits to Teakant's Rainbow and similar establishments on the Dakota trail, Ford had kept the horror locked up in his mind all these years. And then Justin had brought Samantha home.

One day she said, 'Ford, sometimes you seem so sad. Why?'

'Maybe you grow up in the shadow of an older brother. Maybe it's hard to match that, and it makes you sad.'

'I have a feeling it's more than that.' The warmth of her fingers on his wrist cut slowly through the crusty wall he had built against the truth. 'It's something to do with a girl named Elsie. Justin has referred to it obliquely, but he will never talk about it.'

'One day I'll tell you, Samantha.'

'I'm always here to listen to your problems,' she said gently. 'That's what a sister is for.'

She had leaned forward and kissed him on the cheek.

For days afterward he slept fitfully, remembering that kiss.

And now overhead a window slid up in the Rainbow and a girl leaned out into the winter day. 'Ford, are you going away, honey?'

He looked up. 'I'll be back, Helen.'

'I hope so. I miss you.'

* * *

Solly Granger, drinking his Sunday whisky, turned from the saloon window when Ford rode out. 'If he's gone to warn Justin, he won't get far. The first lobo wolf that howls at the winter moon will send him scurrying for home.'

Cob Shandy said, 'Mebby we better make sure that Justin hears about them three fellas.'

'Knowing Justin as I do,' Teakant said, 'you better keep out of it.'

47

CHAPTER SEVEN

One cold morning when they were far uptrail, Justin saw Darsie Polk remove from his pocket the thick Sievers watch that had been passed on to him from his father. The foreman studied the face and grunted, 'Sunrise comes too damn early these days. Loco, that's what it is.' He gave Justin a glance of disapproval. 'Loco.'

'Maybe,' Justin said, and recalled that a cowboy who let them through a gate in the big drift fence across the Panhandle had said the same thing.

'Loco. Never heard of a man drivin' cows nawth this time of year,' the rider had said.

'It's maybe a year for damn fools,' Justin told him.

The fence, many days behind them now, had been his father's last project. Erected to keep northern cattle from drifting into Texas during winter storms, it stretched from Indian Territory's west line a hundred and seventy-five miles to the eastern border of New Mexico. The stout four-wire fence had been started back in '82, the last year of the Major's life. Justin had been against the group, headed by his father, who advocated the fence. He had claimed it was a waste of wire, and would only antagonize the northern ranchers. It was one

48

of the few times he had disagreed with the Major.

Even last evening Darsie Polk said, 'I wish to hell we'd never come through that damn fence and were still down in Texas where a man can freeze in comfort.'

Now on this chill dawn Justin sat up in his blankets under Samantha's wagon. Polk was helping himself to coffee. Orion Smith's wind-burned face was touched by light from his cook fire. Smitty's wife had moved to Midpoint to stay with a sister. She would join her husband at the Ketcher place come spring. The fire threw shadows on the chuckwagon and the freighter loaded with household goods.

Hearing a step, Justin looked around. Samantha, wearing a bearskin coat, stood with one hand held behind her back.

'Justin, do you know what day this is?' she said, her large eyes solemn.

He yawned, shook his head. 'I've lost count.'

'It's Christmas morning.'

He sat up a little straighter. 'Time slips away, that's for sure,' he said, embarrassed that he had overlooked the day.

A hundred yards beyond the camp, the herd, bunched near the entrance to a rock-walled canyon, began to paw into the frosty ground for grass.

Samantha extended her hand. She held a small box wrapped in brown paper, tied with a frayed end of ribbon. 'I didn't have the

49

material with which to do it up fancy. Merry Christmas, Justin.'

A feeling of guilt at his forgetfulness flooded across his face. Thanking her, he took the package and untied the ribbon. Inside was a watch fob, a rim of gold enclosing a twenty-dollar gold piece. Attached to it was a slender gold chain.

'It's very nice,' be said, clearing his throat. 'Really very nice.' He stood up, holding it in his hand to admire it. He didn't know what to say. 'I'm sorry I didn't have a chance to get a present for you. I—'

'I bought it before I left home.' She waited there beside her wagon, her face high with color in the morning cold. From the flats came the off-key voice of a cowhand crooning to edgy cows. Down by the fire, the men were stirring out of their blankets.

Samantha said, 'Are we always going to be apart, Justin?'

He put the watch fob in his pocket. 'We'll make a new life at the Ketcher place.'

'You still believe Ford and I were lovers,' she said despondently.

Pushing a hand through his uncombed hair, he stomped his feet deeper into cold boots. 'I want a new life when we reach Dakota. Away from memories that—'

'Justin, why can't you believe in me?' She took a deep breath and he noticed how her firm breasts stirred under the open bearskin coat. A clutching sensation spread through his chest. He looked away and stared at the desolate land.

'I'm messed up inside,' he said, his voice betraying his own misery. 'Like a tangle of cold rope on an icy morning. But I'll thaw.'

'I wonder.'

'It takes time for a man to get over these things.'

'Justin, soon it will be a new year. I pray it will be a better one for all us Emerys.'

'You include Ford?' he demanded.

'He's your brother. Why shouldn't I wish something good for him?'

Justin laced on his gun rig, not wanting to hurt her on this of all mornings. 'Yes, I hope eighty-six will be a better year.'

When he reached the cook fire Darsie Polk grunted, 'Hell of a way to spend Christmas.'

'Amen,' said Smitty from his cook fire. 'My wife is at her sister's place in Midpoint, with the house warm and smellin' of baked ham and wild turkey.'

'We oughta be at Teakant's,' Darsie Polk murmured, closing his eyes as if he could smell the hot stove and the whisky and bear the laughter of the girls upstairs.

'Next Christmas I'll make it up to all of you,' Justin said awkwardly, wondering if in his rage at Ford he'd had any right to drag these men away from family and friends at Christmas.

Darsie Polk lowered his voice, nodding

toward Samantha, who still stood disconsolately by her wagon. 'Boy, why you got to act so stiff-necked on a morning like this? Go kiss your wife; it's Christmas.'

'Things will be different when we get to Dakota,' Justin said stubbornly.

Polk shook his head. 'Why you always got to wait? You won't make up to your wife, because you got the Major's mule blood in your veins. You won't live now because you got to wait till you can tell them banker boys in Chicago that Justin Emery has one million Yankee dollars in cows and grass.'

'What's wrong with having ambition?' Justin snapped.

'The Major was never satisfied, and neither will you be. He worked himself to death tryin' to be bigger than the next man. Goin' broke, startin' over.' Polk spat into the fire. 'At thirty you'll want five more years, then ten more.'

Justin chewed a warmed-over piece of beef. 'We better get the cows to moving, or we won't make our miles today.'

At sundown they made another camp. Christmas dinner consisted of beans and fried steak. Justin took a tray to Samantha in the wagon. She lay on a pile of blankets, her eyes watching him in the winter twilight.

He thought then how easy it would be to kiss her and be welcomed again to her arms. But some stiff-necked pride made him hold back. He made himself believe that once they reached the Ketcher place things would be different.

'Why can't I penetrate that wall of yours, Justin?' she asked, shifting her legs under the tray that he had placed on her lap. 'If only I could talk with you—'

'I'm a reasonable man and always willing to listen.'

She gave a small laugh there in the shadows under the wagon top. 'Are you really willing to give a person the benefit of a doubt?' Her voice shook. 'Are you willing to believe in those you pretend to love?'

'The less we say about what happened at the Midpoint place the better,' he said gruffly.

'All you can think about is breaking your back against a wheel you hope to turn with all your strength and mind. So that you can become a rich man.'

'You make me sound like a fool. I want the best for us, that's all.'

'Ford told me your father piled dollar upon dollar because it was his only life after his bitter defeat in the war. Do you have your own reasons for putting your life at the foot of a mountain of gold, Justin?'

'You'd better eat your Christmas dinner before it gets cold,' he said, and squeezed her arm, not wanting them to end up in a quarrel again. And in that moment, as he touched her, he was almost lost, so great was his desire to push the ugly scene at the barn down at the

Midpoint place from his mind.

'Samantha,' he said hoarsely.

But she broke the spell, not seeing his face in the quick darkness that shadowed the interior of the wagon. 'You've never forgiven Ford, your own brother, for something that happened years ago,' Samantha said. 'Why should I expect different treatment?'

'The two cases are different,' he snapped, finding the old wound open and festering.

'Ford was twelve years old, a proud boy. He had a boy's infatuation for an older girl.'

'He was warned to stay away from those particular horses.'

'And then when there was no one home one day but Ford and this Elsie, he hitched that team to a wagon.' Samantha's voice grew sad. 'He asked her to take a drive with him because he wanted to show her he could handle the team.'

'Elsie would do anything for Ford. Anything in the world to humor him.' His voice grew thin with a familiar bitterness. 'Just like Momma did before she died.'

'Was that part of Ford's great crime? That he was your mother's favorite, and not you?'

Justin sat rigid in the darkness, hands clamped to his knees.

In a moment Samantha went on, 'Or was his only crime the fact that the team ran away and Elsie Gorman was killed—and Ford lived?'

'Can you excuse what he did, for God's

sake?'

'Not at all. But after all this time, can't you forgive him?'

Forcibly Justin pulled his thoughts away from the day of tragedy. He listened to the sounds of his men, some riding in, others riding out. Muted voices, the clang of a tin cup into a pan.

'Don't you think Ford has lived with that guilt every day of his life?' Samantha said earnestly. 'It's why he turned to whisky. You could have helped him, Justin.' She handed him the tray. 'Take it back. I'm not hungry.'

'I've tried to help Ford many times. He never learned to sit his own saddle.'

'Because you always expect the worst of him.'

Justin cleared his throat, hands clamped to the edges of the metal tray. 'I declare, I believe you're in love with Ford.'

'Can't you distinguish between compassion and love?'

'It's hard for me to get it out of my mind—you and Ford there by the barn. And you with your dress torn.' He set the tray on the blankets, climbed out of the wagon, and hurried down to the cook fire.

Two nights later Darsie Polk said quietly, 'Justin, make it up with your wife.'

Justin ran a hand tiredly over his face. 'I'll come out of this in my own good time.'

Darsie Polk folded the blade of a clasp knife

55

and dropped it into his pocket. He absently kicked through a pile of shavings he had made from whittling on a stick.

'Justin, life is so damned short it sometimes scares a fella. Make it up to your wife.' Flames from the fire leaped toward the black dome of the sky. 'You're both young, but the days slip into months and the months into years.'

'That they do,' Justin agreed, and remembered as if it were only yesterday the day his father came home from Hood's brigade, wearing ragged butternut, a saber slash across his right cheek. The Major shouting that they would fight on, they'd never give up as had that coward Lee.

'It seems like only day before yesterday that I was full of hell and vinegar,' Darsie Polk said. 'Riding up from the Nueces to the Bend with the Major. Then going to war with him, then coming to Midpoint. It's twenty-four years since me and the Major joined up with Hood. The women I loved then are old or dead. I'm old. Don't waste your life, boy.'

Justin felt an edge of stubbornness rise in him like a wall. 'We made good time today,' he said, and looked at the sky. Stars glowed like chips of polished steel, and the only clouds were banked darkly to the east. 'So far, it looks like a mild winter. I have a hunch the good Lord is favoring us.'

Darsie Polk's lips twisted bitterly under the brushy beard. 'You didn't pay attention to one damn thing I said.'

'Darsie, I know what to look for when buying a horse or a mule. I'm not afraid of a fight. I can talk a banker out of money for expansion. But this business of a wife is new. I've got to feel my way.'

'Having a wife is some different than making money in cows.'

'You never bothered to marry,' Justin said sharply. 'So you wouldn't know.'

Polk shrugged off the anger in the younger man's voice. 'Ford's got some strange ideas, and this I freely admit. You fist-fought him and beat him. You should've let that end it, and been man enough to shake his hand.'

'You know the cow business. But when it comes to family problems or a woman, you don't know beans from bear shidd.'

The old man said quietly, 'I never had any family but yours. The Major was always so busy and I was so busy helpin' him, I purely never had the time to find me a wife and settle down under my own roof.'

'I'm sorry for blowing off at you.' Justin slapped the foreman on a thin arm. 'I'll make it up when we get to the Ketcher place.'

'You talk like the Ketcher place is heaven. It's goin' to be no different than Texas. Mebby worse.'

'Will you forgive me for having a spell of being Texas mean?'

Polk gave him a thin smile. 'As the Major

used to say, there ain't no worse meanness a man can get.'

Darsie Polk humped away into the shadows, a stringy man with a sloping shoulder.

CHAPTER EIGHT

The trail north was easy for Erd Quine to follow. Even if they hadn't been able to see the broad fresh path left by the Hayfork cattle, the few settlers were eager to discuss the trail drive. Last night they had taken supper with a shirt-tail rancher named Olman, who said, 'They must be crazy, making a drive north at this time of year. And them with a woman along, too.'

'You saw the woman?' Quine asked quietly over his coffee in the sod house where they were paying to spend the night.

'Seen her?' the rancher's thin-faced wife stormed. 'I'll say he seen her. Lollygagged around the wagon like a schoolboy.'

Olman ignored his wife. 'You fellas aim to help with the drive when you catch up?'

Quine and his two companions exchanged glances. 'We just aim to catch up,' Quine said.

'Hayfork herds been coming through here right regular the last few years,' the rancher said, and got up to shovel buffalo chips into the stove. 'Since Major Emery bought the

58

place up near Ketcher. Mostly it's the young brother Ford who makes the drives. A drinkin' man. Never seen Justin Emery before.' The rancher scraped a dirty fingernail through the stubble of beard that darkened his jaws. 'Struck me as bein' a sour sort of fella.'

'Shouldn't wonder,' Quine observed. 'Personal problems will sometimes do that to a man.'

'With all Emery's money, you wouldn't think he'd have problems,' the woman said sharply. 'All that money and that hussy for a wife.'

'You know for a fact she's a hussy?' Quine said, leaning back in a leather slat chair.

Something in Quine's face caused the woman to tighten her lips. 'I just meant she's a pale-haired woman, and them kind can't be trusted. At least so they say.'

'The rate they're traveling,' the rancher said, leaning forward, 'you oughta catch up in a few days.'

'Probably.'

Quine finished his coffee. The blazing buffalo chips in the unvented room made the place smell like a livery barn on fire. Absently he leaned down, rubbing his fingers across a scar on the calf of his right leg. It had been made by the metal collar of a legiron three years ago when he'd made a brief escape from the Prescott jail. A deputy had winged him in the leg, but he had gotten away in the

59

darkness. For two days he hid out and the leg swelled up around the iron band on his calf. The legiron finally had to be cut off when they recaptured him. The doctor said it was a wonder he hadn't lost the leg.

And Erd Quine had said, 'After I hang, you tell me the difference whether they bury me with one leg or two.'

'You're a bitter man, Quine,' the doctor had said.

And now it was Justin Emery who seemed bitter, according to this raggedy pants cowman in the overheated sod house that smelled of dung.

The rancher was saying, 'What you aim to do when you catch up with Justin Emery, anyhow?'

'Kill him.'

The rancher's jaw fell. 'Kill him?'

'There still are places left where they kill a horsethief,' Erdman Quine said heavily. 'A wife stealer deserves no better treatment.'

'You mean that woman—she's your wife?'

For the rest of the evening, until they rolled up in their blankets, there was an uneasy silence in the sod house. In the morning, after breakfast, Quine paid for their meals and lodging. Then he and his two companions rode north.

When they had cleared the house, with the rancher and his wife staring after them apprehensively, Charlie Ivory shifted his bulk

60

in the saddle. 'Seems to me, Erd, that was a damn fool thing you done—admitting you aim to kill a man.'

Quine looked around at the two riders. He had known Charlie Ivory for some years. Kelso Kane had been accused of attempted murder, rustling and robbery, among other things, but he had never been convicted. He had met Charlie Ivory in Mexico, where both worked for a time as bodyguards at the Yankee-owned Starburst Copper Mines.

'Charlie,' Quine said, 'don't try and give me advice.'

Kelso Kane, astride a dun horse, rode with his lank body hunched in his coat, head down like an Indian. 'You said if we teamed up with you we'd see some money. I ain't seen none yet.'

'You will,' Quine said.

They rode in silence, the hoofs of their horses rapping sharply against the frosty ground.

As the day's chill deepened, Erd Quine thought of Yuma Prison, where a man would be tempted to cut off his fingers one at a time in exchange for an hour of icy wind in his face.

In those years the greatest blow was being deprived of his wife. He thought of their wedding night, with Samantha lying deep in the oversized feather bed, all golden and warm, and her whisper against his throat, 'A new life, Erd—for us both.'

A new life.

The judge saying sternly, 'Because of the memory of your late father, the jury has spared you. Instead of hanging, you are to spend the rest of your natural life behind the walls of the prison at Yuma.'

Quine had turned on the jury, his lips white. 'It would have been more merciful to hang me.'

Despite the cold, Quine was sweating. He shoved a hand under his leather coat to feel the grips of a revolver. He had never heard Justin Emery's name until one day at the oaken bar in the Empire Hotel, St. Louis, when a man answered the question Quine had asked so often. 'Why, yes, I remember Samantha well. She married a man named Emery. Justin Emery. He's a cattleman somewhere out in Texas.'

Now Quine removed the hand from the grips of his revolver, frowning. There was something too merciful in a revolver shot. It was the way you killed a horse with a broken leg, or a favorite dog gone suddenly mad.

Two nights later, at a trading post, he dickered with the owner of a shotgun with shortened barrels. When the deal was consummated, Kelso Kane said, 'Why the shotgun?'

'It's the way to obliterate the face of a thief.' Quine ground his teeth together. 'Nothing left for a woman to weep over. Nothing at all.'

'With a shotgun it's awful quick killin',' said Ivory.

'If we have the chance, maybe I'll let you knock him around a little, Charlie.'

'It's hard to hold back in a fight with a man you don't figure to kill.'

'This time you hold back when I tell you,' Quine said.

CHAPTER NINE

As the days passed Justin's luck seemed to hold. Ice had not formed on the rivers to any great extent, although the cows fought against being driven into the freezing waters. Justin and his men made the crossings, losing only a few head.

Purposely, Justin had skirted the Kansas border, and luckily he found no Kansans brandishing guns and ordering him back because the cattle had ticks. This had happened to earlier drives this year. Maybe you couldn't blame the Kansas boys too much, Justin conceded. There was bad blood between the northern outfits and the Texans. There always had been, for that matter, but it was compounded now by the drift fence across the Panhandle. The fence didn't set well with the Kansans.

One noon it turned almost warm. Justin,

riding at point, unbuttoned his jacket.

Smitty, driving the chuckwagon, grinned at him. 'I declare, it feels 'most like spring,' he called. 'You got the Major's luck, for sure.'

'Let's hope the luck holds.'

'Yep, we're goin' to make it—make it without freezin' solid to saddle or wagon seat.'

Justin suddenly had an idea. He'd hardly spoken to Samantha since the night at her wagon when she'd brought up the ugly business of Ford and Elsie, and what had happened later at the barn down at the Midpoint place. Her attempts to defend Ford had galled him.

But now he slanted over to her wagon, which was being driven by a lame cowhand named Pete Shagrue.

Samantha saw him coming and put her head out the canvas flaps at the rear of the wagon. 'It's warm,' she said.

He nodded. 'Tired?'

'A little.' The shawl she usually wore over her golden hair now hung about her shoulders. 'I'm surprised you'd honor me with a visit.'

'Smitty just said it's most like spring. Mexia Springs is just ahead, according to Darsie. I— I'll have Pete drive the wagon over. I'd like you to pick yourself out a gift. Something I should have done for Christmas.'

'But, Justin, I don't need—'

Leaning over in the saddle, he pressed a ten-dollar gold piece into her hand. Then he swung to the front of the wagon to give Pete Shagrue his orders.

Mexia Springs was a collection of dugouts and frame buildings. The main structure was Hearn's Store, which featured a bar, well-stocked shelves, a counter, some deal tables scattered around a huge stove. In the back of the store were six rooms for lodgers.

Samantha entered the store and instantly noted the silence from the men gathered about the stove. It was an old and familiar story to her. She paid no attention to the men. For some minutes she browsed, looking at bolts of material, enjoying the warmth of the store. Pete Shagrue lounged in the wagon with the Hayfork brand prominently displayed on the sideboard facing the store.

A stooped man behind the counter, wearing bib overalls, came up. Samantha asked if she could see some scarves. The man seemed ill at ease. He kept licking his lips and glancing nervously toward the shadowed rear of the store.

She picked out a scarf of pale yellow to match her hair. 'I'll take this one,' she said, and laid the ten-dollar gold piece on the counter.

'That'll be a dollar, Mrs. Quine.'

She was reaching for the scarf, intending to put it in the pocket of her heavy coat. Then she froze. 'You called me *Mrs. Quine!*' she said hoarsely.

'Ain't that your name?'

Suddenly she felt an old familiar terror. Snatching the ten-dollar gold piece from the counter, she rushed out into the winter afternoon. Pete Shagrue looked at her in surprise.

'Get me away from here,' she whispered, climbing into the wagon.

Behind his counter, Joe Hearn picked up the yellow scarf and returned it to the box. He saw the wagon drive off.

When Erd Quine came out of a back room, smiling, Hearn gave him a thin look. 'She turned white,' Hearn said. 'Dead white.'

'I told you she would.' Quine laughed. Then he looked across the room where Charlie Ivory and Kane were sitting against the wall in tipped-back chairs. 'Are you disappointed in her?'

'A fine figure of a woman,' Charlie Ivory said.

And when Kelso Kane made no reply, Quine said, 'Isn't she everything I said she was?'

Kane gave Quine a flat stare. 'A man might find it hard to keep his brand on a woman like that.'

'Don't you get any notions of changing that brand, Kelso,' Quine warned.

Charlie Ivory set down his chair on the floor. 'Kelso's stole about everything else, but he don't steal women.' Ivory tried to lessen the tense moment with a laugh. 'That right, Kelso?'

'That's right,' Kelso said, but he was staring off at the tail end of the Hayfork wagon he could barely see through the trees that ringed Mexia Springs. The wagon left deep tracks in last week's dirty snow.

CHAPTER TEN

Justin, riding at drag, was surprised to see the wagon return so soon from Mexia Springs. He rode over and stood up in the stirrups while he pushed aside the canvas flaps and peered in.

'Did you get yourself a present?' he asked, smiling in at Samantha. She lay on the blankets, hardly visible in the shadowed interior of the wagon.

'I feel ill,' she said, a forearm across her eyes. 'Please leave me alone.'

Something about her voice worried him. He tried to question her, while he kept his mount at a walk at the rear of the wagon, but she refused to say any more.

Frowning, Justin rode to the front of the wagon and gave Pete Shagrue a questioning glance. Pete only shrugged, to indicate he didn't know what it was that might be troubling Samantha.

When they made camp in an hour, Justin

got Shagrue aside. 'Pete, what happened at the springs?'

'I dunno. She went in Hearn's Store, and right away she come runnin' out as if somebody had set her skirts afire. I never seen a woman so pale.'

Justin said, 'Don't mention it to her. And don't say anything about it to anybody else.'

Justin caught up a fresh horse. Darsie Polk said, 'Where you goin', Justin?'

'Back to Hearn's Store.'

'Now if you was Ford, I'd say you figured to buy yourself a jug of whisky. But—'

'I'll be back directly,' Justin snapped, cutting his foreman off.

It was full dark when he reached the store. A few saddlers were being sheltered in the big barn adjoining the store. Lights glowed from the windows of a handful of dugouts behind the store.

When Justin stepped into Hearn's Store, he glanced around, easing his revolver in its holster under his coat. Seven or eight men lounged around a big stove, tipped back in chairs, feet on a low iron railing. In the dim glow of wall lamps he couldn't distinguish faces. Behind the counter a man wearing bib overalls looked up from a ledger where he was copying figures.

Justin said, 'Were you here this afternoon, in the store?'

'Reckon.'

'I'm Justin Emery.'

'Heard of you, Mr. Emery. Your brother stops in when he comes nawth.'

'My wife was here this afternoon. Something frightened her. I want to know what happened.'

Hearn tried to pick up the ledger from the counter, but his hand shook so he dropped it. 'Don't blame me,' be said, swallowing. 'I never had nothing to do with it.'

Suddenly a very large man got up from one of the chairs across the room. The other men stared as the big one skirted the stove on his ponderous way to the counter.

Justin looked around. The big man was grinning. He was a head taller than Justin, and thick through the shoulders. His nose was flat, his brows scarred. A deep scar puckered his right cheek. Still grinning, he removed a heavy coat and laid it on the counter.

'So you're Justin Emery?' he said.

'And who are you?' Justin demanded gruffly.

'I'm a fella who don't like you, Mr. Emery.'

Before Justin could set himself, the big man suddenly lashed out with a fist. Instinctively Justin turned his head. Instead of the full force of the powerful blow landing on his jaw, it struck his shoulder. The impact spun him, drove him against the counter.

As Justin hung there for a moment the big man closed in, arms spread wide to trap him.

But Justin ducked, took a backward step. He drew his gun with such suddenness that the big man froze. Others in the room hurriedly left their chairs. They flattened themselves against the far wall, to get as far as possible from the zone of trouble, yet near enough to witness whatever might transpire.

Gripping the gun in a solid fist, Justin said, 'I don't know who you are, and I don't care. But if you're the one who insulted my wife, just bear this in mind. Don't do it again, or I'll kill you. And I mean that.'

Justin let his gaze flick about the room. He saw faces watching him in the dim lamplight. Slowly he backed to the door and holstered his revolver. 'Remember what I said.'

No one followed him out of the store. All the way back to camp he tried to decide what had put such terror in Samantha. The sudden pointless attack by the big stranger was unsettling. He could have stayed and tried to force from him the reason for the attack, but he sensed that the man had friends at the store. It could have ended up in a shooting. The town was no place for a man to be alone, especially when he didn't know what had provoked the hostility against him.

Samantha wasn't at the fire when Justin rode in. Darsie Polk said, 'Justin, I got a bad feelin' of trouble.' He glanced at the sky. 'I still say it's a bad time of year for a drive.'

'We'll get through,' Justin said from force of

habit.

Using a piece of gunnysack to hold the coffee pot, he filled his cup, debating how best to get Samantha to tell him the truth of what had happened back at Mexia Springs. In the darkness he could see the massive silhouette of his herd. He could almost sense their nervousness. Any overt sound, a boot stepping on a stick, the snuffle of a horse, would cause them to jerk up their heads and stare. The farther north they came the more sensitive the cattle seemed to their environment.

A silence touched the camp. Justin turned his head and saw Samantha coming down from her wagon, golden hair loose, a shawl about her shoulders.

On this strange night with the almost-spring warmth in the air, she seemed more serenely beautiful than ever. Sight of her sent a tug of longing through him. Was he, after all, a damn fool? Was Darsie Polk right about the years passing so swiftly? He remembered how she had stood out in the crowded lobby of the Empire Hotel. In a land of beautiful women, she had been supreme. At least so she had seemed to him.

As she approached, the men gathered by the cook fire seemed transfixed. She spoke to them and some said, 'Howdy, Ma'am,' or, 'Evenin', Mrs. Emery.'

Samantha turned to Justin. 'Do you realize it's nearly the last of the old year?'

71

Justin nodded and got her a plate of food. She seemed to have recovered from whatever had troubled her at Mexia Springs. However, he couldn't be sure; she had a way of holding things within herself.

As they ate the same beef and beans they'd had for days now, Darsie Polk threw more wood on the fire.

Flames shooting high into the still air showered sparks. Justin sat beside his wife on a deadfall. He said quietly, 'Now you can tell me what happened in town today.'

For a moment she sat stiffly, staring at the fire. Then she said, 'A man called me Mrs. Quine.'

Justin's shoulders stiffened; then he shrugged. 'Well, what's so strange about that? He probably recognized you from the old days, before you married me.'

'I don't think so.' She put her plate on the ground beside her booted feet. She wore canvas breeches and a wool shirt. Her heavy coat was slung over her shoulders. 'I think it was something else.'

The men sat some distance away. Justin listened to them discussing the close of '85 and the approach of '86, so near at hand; how the move to Dakota would change all their lives. Once there had been a time when a man would be hard put to leave Texas. But a lot of them were doing it now; the horizons of the cattle business were broadening. On this drive,

Justin was constantly reminded how the country was growing. He'd made the trip north to the Ketcher place only once, and that by steam cars to Chicago and then to Dakota by horseback. It was when the Major first bought the new ranch. It had been Ford's responsibility to stock the northern range with Texas Hayfork cattle. The job had been done, with no thanks to Ford, who admittedly spent his time on the trail with a bottle or with various girls.

Darsie Polk put a foot on the deadfall and sipped coffee. 'Another year and there'll be so many new roads and fences the cattle drives will be finished,' the foreman said dolefully.

'A sad thing,' Justin agreed.

Perhaps next year the government would get around to recognizing the cattle industry as a business of such magnitude that it could have a direct bearing on the economy of the nation. It was time the government stopped listening to the railroads and for a change gave an ear to needs of the cattlemen—such as appropriate legislation for a permanent national cattle trail; land set aside to provide a roadway from Texas to the northern ranges. If such a trail were not soon developed, the prophecy of Darsie Polk would come to pass. The days of the big drives would be over. That point had been stressed many times during heated exchanges at the St. Louis convention last year.

Despite the furor, the issue had been left in the air. It seemed inconceivable to Justin that there might come a time when cattle would no longer be driven from one range to another. For twenty years Texas cows had been streaming north, first to Missouri and Abilene, then the later shipping points. But this could end if the cattlemen didn't get together to press their representatives in Washington for the settlement of the issue of a cattle trail.

When Darsie Polk wandered back to the fire, Justin picked up Samantha's plate. 'You'd better eat.' He tried to force the plate on her, but she had turned her head to stare at him, firelight touching her eyes.

Suddenly she gripped his wrists. 'Listen to me, Justin,' she said in a hoarse whisper. 'I have something to confess. Something I should have told you a long time ago.'

He drew back, a withering sickness spreading under his heart. 'That day at the barn. You and Ford—'

She gave a quick shake of her head. 'Is that all you can think about?' She sat back, removing her hands from his wrists. 'I don't suppose you would believe me, no matter what I said. You won't listen to me. Your whole mind is filled with your brother and that day by the barn.'

She broke off. Her voice had carried. The men made a great show of pretending they hadn't heard. Darsie Polk had drawn out his

74

Sievers watch and was gazing fondly at it. He tilted it so firelight touched the Roman numerals.

'As my Poppa's watch says,' Polk said, 'it is now seven o'clock of a winter night. No matter how warm it may seem, boys,' he went on, snapping shut the case of the stem winder, 'she's now dead winter.'

The sound of slow-moving horses cut through the stillness. Orion Smith said, 'Company comin'.'

Polk returned the watch to his pocket. 'Let's hope they ride up easy and don't set them cows to runnin'.'

Justin was on his feet, facing north in the direction of the sound. 'Easy!' he shouted. 'Don't do anything to spook our cows.'

'We come fair quiet,' an old man's voice said out of the night.

In a few moments two riders appeared from the shadows, astride shaggy horses. They wore short buffalo coats over dirty buckskins. Something out of the past, mountain men.

'Light,' Justin invited. 'You're welcome to eat with us.'

'Thankee kindly, but we done et,' said a gray-bearded man. 'Took on a bellyful of food at Princess Station, a few miles ahead on the Coldwell Road. You oughta reach it tomorrow.'

'Spread your blankets,' Justin suggested as the pair dismounted.

75

'Might take some coffee,' the old man muttered. 'We'll rest a mite, then push on. It's a time for headin' south.' He stripped off a glove and put out his hand to Justin. 'Name of Mitch DeForrest.' When he and Justin had shaken hands, DeForrest jerked a thumb at his companion, a black-haired man of middle years. 'Eddie Wolfnose. He's part Kiowa.'

Eddie Wolfnose only grunted and squatted on the ground. He accepted the cup of coffee Smitty handed him. DeForrest helped himself.

Darsie Polk had been standing in the shadows of the chuckwagon. Now he came up, slowly, staring at the two men. Polk sank to the deadfall near Justin, across from the halfbreed.

'You part Kiowa, huh?' Polk said.

'Big part Kiowa,' Eddie Wolfnose said, and laughed. Then the laugh faded and he lifted his head and stared straight into Darsie Polk's eyes: He said, 'Why you look at me that way?'

Mitch DeForrest laughed: 'Don't pay no attention to Eddie. He's always thinkin' some white man's got a long memory for scalp knives.'

DeForrest rambled on about the country to the north. He and the Kiowa had been working the upper Missouri. The pelts were not as easy come by as in the old days. Cattlemen up there were scaring out a lot of game.

'Hunted buffler for a spell, till they was

killed off,' DeForrest said. His gaze kept swinging to Samantha, who still sat on the deadfall. Then he would look at the sky. 'You better turn tail an' head back for Texas,' he told Justin. 'Bad winter comin'.'

Eddie Wolfnose nodded in agreement, still looking at Darsie. 'Bad, bad,' he grunted.

'You ever been in Texas?' Darsie Polk asked the Kiowa.

Eddie Wolfnose finished his coffee and wiped his lips on the back of his hand. 'No Texas,' he said.

'You ever have kinfolks down there?'

'Maybe.'

Darsie Polk was nervously winding his watch with a small silver crank. The Kiowa seemed interested. He put out his hand.

'Fine watch,' Eddie Wolfnose said.

Darsie Polk hesitated a moment, then handed over the watch. 'My father give it to me. I—I think a lot of it.'

'Watch tell pretty time,' the Kiowa said, squinting at the Roman numerals on the face, which he obviously didn't understand. 'They say one time my people hungry, they starve. A watch like this buy much food.'

Darsie Polk suddenly got to his feet. 'Keep the watch,' he said in a voice taut with strain. Everybody looked at him in surprise. 'It—it's a present.'

Polk hurried away into the darkness, caught up a horse and rode out to where the herd was

77

being held by the rest of the crew.

Mitch DeForrest was staring after the foreman. 'Mebby he don't like the way me an' Eddie smell. He sure lit a shuck outa here.'

The Kiowa had the watch pressed to his ear, enjoying the sounds. Justin held out his hand. 'Give it to me. Darsie must be drunk. He's either got a bottle hid in his blankets, or he's all of a sudden gone crazy.'

'The watch mine now,' Eddie Wolfnose said.

'Darsie'd sooner cut off an arm than part with that watch.'

Mitch DeForrest seemed to be turning the situation over in his mind. He glanced around at Justin's armed camp. 'We met loco gents before this, Eddie. Give him back the watch.'

Reluctantly the Kiowa returned the watch. Justin handed it to Smitty. 'Keep it for Darsie. When he rides in, see that he gets it.'

Smitty nodded and put the watch in one of the compartments at the tailgate of the chuckwagon.

Justin turned, to find Samantha watching him, arms rigid at her sides. He came up to her, saying, 'Don't look at me that way. What have I done to you?'

'You—you're such a fair man in most things. You make that man give back Darsie's watch. But when it comes to me or to Ford—' her voice broke— 'I just can't reach you at all.'

He said awkwardly, 'I truly believe things will change at Ketcher. Will you bear with me

78

till then?'

But she was already hurrying up the slant to her wagon. Justin caught up with her and tried to take her arm, but she was weeping and refused even to speak to him. He did help her into the wagon, but she dropped the canvas flaps in his face and began to lace them hastily against the night air.

At last, when he could not get her to answer him, he returned to the fire, feeling small and mean. What had he said or done to upset her this time? He felt his shoulder where the big man at Hearn's Store had struck him. He should have forced her to tell him what it was that had upset her so. But she had seemed overwrought and in no condition to bear up under his questioning.

When he neared the fire he heard DeForrest say to Smitty, 'Now I've seen some prime females in my time, but not one that quite stirs the blood.'

Smitty gave Justin, standing there in the shadows, a nervous glance.

'DeForrest, she's my wife.' Justin said coldly.

The old man twisted around, spilling his coffee over the dirty buckskins. 'Beggin' your pardon. I figured she was—' He broke off, then went on lamely, 'Just a woman traveling with you.'

After a moment of uncomfortable silence, DeForrest jerked his head at the Kiowa. They

79

got their horses and mounted up. 'Be a bad winter, you mark me,' DeForrest said. 'And I didn't mean no offense about your wife. Just sorta squeezed off my breath, seein' a looker like her at this fringe of the devil's icy beard.'

When they had gone, Justin rode out to where Darsie Polk sat his saddle, staring at the rim of shadows beyond the camp.

'What in hell got into you, Darsie?' Justin demanded. 'You acted like the breed had jabbed you with a hot pin.'

'Wanted to be alone. Still do.' He looked around at Justin significantly.

'There's a reason for you running like that. What is it?'

For a moment Polk only sat slumped in the saddle. Beyond, the herd stirred restlessly. 'Always get nervous around a red man. Specially a Kiowa.'

'He's only part Kiowa, according to DeForrest.'

'Part or whole, it makes no difference.' Polk looked around. 'Voices carry on a night like this. I couldn't help hear what was said about Samantha.'

'He knew damn well I didn't like it.'

'You're goin' to end up with a bad stomach,' the foreman grunted, 'if you don't quit boilin' every time a man notices your wife.'

'If we get an early start in the morning,' Justin said, 'maybe you and me can sneak over to Princess Station and get ourselves a drink to celebrate the coming of eighteen eighty-six.'

'One of us better stay with the herd. Bad winter comin', so DeForrest said.'

'Mountain men are full of superstitions.'

'Justin, I wish you'd put the missus on a stage at the station. Be a lot easier on us all if we didn't have her to worry about in case somethin' goes wrong.'

Justin crossed his forearms on the saddlehorn. 'Darsie, with all my other troubles, now I've got you to worry about.'

'What you mean? And what's that got to do with puttin' Samantha on a stage?'

'She stays with us. What I mean is this: Why'd you give the Kiowa your watch?'

'Why'd you wait till now to ask, if it's so all-fired important?'

'Thought maybe you'd tell me yourself.'

Polk gestured into the darkness. 'I got my own reasons. Besides, it's my business. It's my watch and I do what I please with it.'

'I got it back for you. Smitty's holding it.'

Darsie Polk twisted in the saddle. His teeth were bared behind the matting of whiskers. His beard seemed completely white now. 'You had no right to do that,' he said, his voice shaking.

Before Justin could say anything more, the old man rode off into the darkness. But Justin did add, to his retreating figure, 'You're touchy as a cat astride barbed wire.'

CHAPTER ELEVEN

In her wagon, Samantha listened to the talk drifting up from the cook fire. She heard Princess Station mentioned. If the weather held, some of them might be able to go over to the station and get a drink. Samantha knew that she could manage to have Pete Shagrue hold back the wagon behind the herd. She would plead illness or make some other excuse. Then she would have Shagrue drive her to the station. When a stage came she'd take it, no matter where it went, just so she got out of Justin's life. It was only fair.

For weeks now she had made herself believe that Mary Hope's letter from St. Louis did not state facts, but was only the result of her old friend's listening to idle gossip and becoming alarmed. But she knew the truth now. Erd was free. Today proved it. It was the sort of thing he'd do. She knew him so well. *Mrs. Quine.*

She squeezed her eyes shut in the lonely bed of the wagon and felt hot tears spill across her cheeks. Knowing in her own heart that Erd was a free man numbed her.

She sensed him to be nearby, toying with her. This knowledge that he might be a mile or ten miles away, after all this time, only made her more determined than ever to cut herself free of Justin. At least Justin should be spared.

Her only reaction to Erd now was a sort of wonderment that she had been such a fool as not to recognize that his good looks were only a façade to mask a pool of corruption. It seemed so incredibly long ago that she had first seen him on the streets of Paso and he had said, 'May I have the honor one day of calling upon you?'

If only she had turned her back on him then.

Had that happened she probably would never have met Justin. The past year of her life with Justin had made up for what had gone before; it was her only happiness.

Perhaps had her father lived he would have been able to view Erd Quine with male objectivity and see the rascality in him. But her father had died in the first year of the war, twenty-four years ago, months before her birth. A colonel, he had been sitting in his tent, writing an account of the First Manassas, when he was struck by a Union shell in the last moments of that battle.

She and her mother remained in St. Louis during the war. When Samantha was sixteen her mother remarried and they made the arduous journey to Paso Del Norte, where the new husband was in business. It was soon plain to Samantha that it was interest, not in a new wife, but in a stepdaughter, that motivated Amos Lark. A friend of her mother's, Muriel LePage, wrote from Chihuahua City that she

83

would welcome Samantha as a companion. Samantha spent two years with the LePages. But John LePage fell into temporary disfavor with Diaz, and they were forced to flee Mexico.

Samantha knew she had to make something of her life. She had no desire to return home, because of her stepfather. Determined to be self-sufficient, she had taken employment for a time as a governess, in Paso. It was there she met Erdman Quine. His courtship was skilled and fervent, and she decided she should marry him.

It was not long before she realized that he was a thief and worse. Soon she became known around Prescott as 'that slut who married old Ches Quine's no-good son.'

Now, in the darkness of the wagon, she reaffirmed her vow to get away, perhaps go to Denver or back to Mexico. She had already involved Justin enough. She would not involve him further.

CHAPTER TWELVE

In the morning Smitty got Justin aside and said, 'Darsie acts mad as hell. He won't take the watch back.'

Justin gave a weary shake of his head. 'He does act loco, for sure. Well, forget him. We've

84

got problems enough as it is.'

Only once during the drive that day did Samantha speak to him. When he rode close to the wagon, as he had done on several occasions, he was happy to see that this time the flaps were pushed aside.

She leaned out, her face grave. 'How far are we from Princess Station?' she asked.

'According to my figures we'll be a couple of miles from it when we camp tonight. Maybe less.' He pushed his horse nearer the wagon. 'Maybe you could ride over with me tomorrow. Do you good to see people.'

'We'll see, Justin.' She leaned back into the wagon and closed the flaps.

That night darkness came so suddenly Justin was forced to make camp near a road that angled through a stand of cedars. Patches of new snow lay upon the ground. It was risky being this close to a road, with the cows restless as they were. But he couldn't push on after dark. They'd just have to hope there wouldn't be much travel on the road this time of year.

A light drizzle fell, then tapered off. At supper Justin tried to draw Samantha out concerning the episode at Mexia Springs. But she countered by asking him about the condition of the house at the Ketcher place.

'If the roof leaks, we'll fix it, that's for sure,' Justin promised.

She only picked at her food. He was

beginning to worry about her. Finally he had to bring it out into the open. 'Listen, Samantha,' he said in a low voice. 'At Hearn's Store a big man tried to pick a fight. Is he the one who frightened you?'

She looked puzzled. 'No, it wasn't anyone like that.'

'Then what is it?'

'I'm just tired of discussions, of trying to make myself believed.' She lifted a hand in a gesture of despair. 'I'm just tired, that's all.'

Something in her tone kindled resentment. 'Are you trying to turn things about now? To blame me about Ford?'

'Stop it, Justin. I don't want to hear any more.'

He ate in silence. The men were not talkative tonight. Justin felt spent, not at all sure his decision to come north at this time of year had been wise. He'd really had a spell of what the Major used to call being 'Texas mean'.

Again he tried to ease the rift between them. 'I'll hire carpenters, Samantha, if I have to send clear to Chicago. I want to remake the house at Ketcher just the way you want it.'

Her shadowed face turned to his in surprise. 'Why, Justin, what a nice thing for you to say.'

Justin felt a lift of spirits. He was reaching for her hand when he heard a sound in the darkness that brought every cow lumbering to its feet.

The sound came with nerve-jarring suddenness from the road.

'What in the hell is that!' cried Darsie Polk.

Justin shot an uneasy glance at the herd, circled by some of his men. The sound came again from some distance away in the crisp night air. He could hear the cows beginning to stir.

'Some fool's too damn lazy to grease his wagon proper,' Justin said, identifying the sound at last.

'That's the trouble with this country,' Darsie Polk said sourly. 'Each trip north a man finds roads where cowpaths used to be.'

Screech—screech—screech.

'Darsie, you and the boys keep an eye on the herd,' Justin snapped. 'I'll go see what kind of hombre drives a squeaky wagon after dark.'

He caught Samantha by an arm and hustled her to the wagon. Ten feet beyond, a rock-strewn hill, covered with patchy snow, rose sharply into the darkness.

'If there's trouble,' he told her, 'get up there. Out of the way.' Impulsively he kissed her and heard her gasp of surprise. Then he caught up a horse and was heading east along the road.

He'd ridden only a short distance, the sound closer now, when he saw a yellow running-light of some sort. Then he saw it was a lantern hanging on a wagon sideboard. It threw pale light over a man on a high seat. He could see

87

the man's long coat. It was yellow-striped. Sharing the seat was what looked like a boy.

As Justin appeared in the cone of light the driver hauled in a team of mules. He grunted in surprise. 'What do you want?' he demanded querulously. He wrapped the lines quickly around the brake handle and tried to reach for a rifle.

'Easy there,' Justin called. 'I mean you no harm. But your wagon's liable to spook my cattle.' He explained that his herd was already jumpy, bedded not a quarter of a mile down the road. The Hayfork cook fire glimmered across the clearing.

'You cowmen don't own the country these days.' Thick burnsides gave a fuzzy width to the man's rather handsome, narrow face. His mouth was thinned down, suspicious. An odor of raw whisky hung in the night air.

Justin flicked a glance to the other occupant of the seat, realizing now that it was not a boy, but a dark-haired girl. She wore Levis and boots and a heavy jacket that hung open.

'Uncle Jethro,' she warned the driver, 'now don't make trouble.' Then she leaned toward Justin. 'This is Jethro Karns, and I'm Ivy. We're trying to reach Princess Station on the Coldwell Road.'

Justin touched his hatbrim. 'Miss Ivy, I'm afraid the noise of your wagon tonight will—'

'Why'd you bed your herd down so close to the road, then?' Jethro Karns demanded.

The girl put a restraining hand on Karns' arm. She seemed quite young, and her voice was soft. Now she smiled at Justin in the lantern light.

'If my uncle drives slowly, will that be all right?'

Justin shook his head. 'Can't risk it, ma'am. Slow or fast, the squeak is still there. I have axle grease at camp, and I can have some of my men—?'

'Things have changed up here,' Karns said brusquely. 'You cowmen have no right to block this road.'

'You and your niece are welcome to make camp with us tonight,' Justin stated flatly. 'My wife can see to the girl's comfort.'

Karns looked surly. When Ivy opened her mouth to speak, he told her to shut up. 'Got a valuable cargo,' he said. 'Figure to reach the station tonight.' He was turned in the seat, gesturing toward his load under a lashed-down tarp.

Suddenly he whipped around, drawing a gun from under the yellow-striped coat. The girl screamed. Although Justin couldn't reach the man's weapon, he was close enough to seize Karns by an arm. At the same moment Justin neck-reined his horse. The force of the move jerked Karns off the seat. He somersaulted, dropping the pocket revolver. It jarred against a wheel hub and exploded a shot into the darkness.

89

Darsie Polk's shout came from a distance. 'Justin, you in trouble?'

'Stay there, Darsie. Watch the herd!' Justin looked around. 'Can you hold those mules, miss?'

'They won't run,' she assured him.

Justin made sure they wouldn't run by tightening the wrapped lines around the brake handle. He saw the girl holding both hands to her mouth, her dark eyes wide. 'Uncle Jethro shouldn't have attempted to draw on a man like you. I never saw anyone move so fast in my life.'

Justin swung down. Karns lay on his side, gasping for breath. The wind had been knocked out of him. Justin hauled him to his feet.

'This settles it,' Justin said sternly. 'You'll both camp with us tonight.'

'You got no right!' Karns spluttered.

At that moment Darsie Polk rode up. 'Wonder them cows didn't run,' the foreman said sourly. He glared at Karns. 'What's this all about?'

Tersely Justin explained the situation. 'The wagon stays here for the night. Darsie, send Pete Shagrue out to guard it.'

Polk rode back in the direction of the Hayfork camp to send out Shagrue.

Then Justin helped the girl down from the wagon. Her arms were slender and soft. When she swayed to the ground, her coat flying open, she felt warm and vital against him. Her dark hair briefly touched his face.

'This will be fun,' she murmured, looking up at him as he tied the mules to a tree. 'I was tired of riding in the wagon. You sound Texan. What's your name?'

He told her. 'I'm on my way to my ranch up in Dakota.'

'A real Texas rancher.' Ivy seemed impressed. 'They say some of you are so rich your spurs are solid gold.'

'Not this rancher.' And he laughed. For the first time in weeks the laughter came easy. He said, 'Come on.' He gave Karns a nudge. 'We'll walk to camp. It isn't far.'

As Karns started out, head down, he grumbled, 'I still say this is high-handed.'

'Uncle Jethro, you could see his side of it if you'd try,' said Ivy.

'You'd better mind your business, dear Ivy, or come tomorrow—' Karns' warning faded when he saw Justin looming above him. He hurried away toward camp.

Justin led his horse, with Ivy clinging to his arm. Once she held to his arm with both hands so he could swing her across a narrow stream. He felt the hard point of a small breast against his arm.

Karns grumbled again. 'That's a valuable cargo I have back there.'

'You have my word that it will be safe.'

'I take Mr. Emery's word, Uncle Jethro,' Ivy

91

said. 'So should you.'

'You should learn to keep your wagon greased,' Justin said to Karns.

'Uncle Jethro had another wagon,' Ivy cut in, 'but it was wrecked. Some cowboys—' She didn't finish it.

'Some hell-raisers?' Justin asked.

Karns gave a snort. 'I see you have a label for your own kind. I had to pay double to get this wagon. It is old and rusted and I didn't have time to worry about greasing axles.'

'How long will you stay in Dakota, Mr. Emery?' Ivy asked.

'From now on, I reckon.' Justin told her how they would swim cattle across the Missouri in the spring and make for the railroad at Amestoy Junction for shipment to Chicago.

'It must be a wonderful city,' she exclaimed. 'Will your wife go with you?'

'You never know about women,' he said, shrugging. 'Some of them like to stick pretty close to home.'

'I'd go anywhere with my husband if he wanted me to.' She spoke wistfully.

Somehow her nearness eased some of the tiredness, the frustrations that had been boiling up in Justin on the drive. And this ending of one year, the approach of a new one, could not help but have a mellowing effect.

At camp, Justin explained the situation to Samantha, who stood woodenly beside her wagon.

'The girl is welcome, of course,' Samantha said in a dead voice.

Ivy turned to Karns, her eyes shining. 'Just think, Uncle Jethro, if those cowboys hadn't wrecked the other wagon, we would never had met Mr. Emery.' And then she added, 'And Mr. Emery's fine wife.'

'I still say it's banditry,' Karns snapped, 'holding a man up this way.' He glared at Justin.

'In the morning we'll get the herd on the move,' Justin said. 'Out of earshot of your squeaky wagon.'

Darsie Polk came up and said, 'I sent Pete Shagrue to feed the mules and keep an eye on the outfit.'

When Justin rode in at midnight from first watch, he saw that Karns was rolled up in a blanket someone had loaned him, sleeping by the fire.

Justin started for the chuckwagon to help himself to some coffee. He was surprised to find Samantha standing there. She held out a cup of hot coffee to him.

'You should be in bed,' he said softly, taking the cup.

'The girl seems exhausted. I let her have my bed.' Samantha lowered her gaze. 'I just wanted to be with you on this last night.'

'You mean the last night of the old year?' He sipped the strong coffee. 'You're a day early. The last day of eighty-five is tomorrow.'

'So it is,' Samantha said.

'I feel sorry for the girl. She seems so alone. I don't care for her uncle.'

'She says her name is Hollister. She claims her aunt lives somewhere to the west. She was rather vague about the exact location.'

Something in Samantha's voice compelled him to defend the girl. 'So she's traveling with Karns, who doesn't happen to be her blood uncle. What of it? There are worse things.' He saw Samantha flinch and thought, Now why did I have to go and say that?

'I'll go to bed now,' she said, and he had to hurry to catch up to her.

When he tried to explain that he had meant nothing personal by the remark, she only shrugged. He helped her into the wagon.

Ivy's sleepy voice said, 'Who is it? Oh, it's you, Mrs. Emery. Here, I'll make room.'

CHAPTER THIRTEEN

Darsie Polk awakened before dawn on this, the last day of 1885. It would be a bad day, Darsie Polk felt. God knew it had been a bad night. He hadn't been able to get that Kiowa, Eddie Wolfnose, out of his mind.

Perhaps it was because they had been too long on the trail and were thin at the nerve ends. A man began to imagine things.

94

Polk recalled how the Kiowa had looked directly at him, the dark eyes seeming to bore through blood and flesh and reach the soul of one D. W. Polk. Imagination, sure; what else? Try as he would, however, Polk couldn't deny the feeling of guilt that had ridden him for so long.

Years back, right after the war, he and the Major had gone after some horsethieves. Comanches; Polk was sure of that. He knew Indian sign.

After some miles of trailing the fugitives, they met a Captain Ellspeth and two of his men. Ellspeth had also lost horses. He was traveling with a wagon, which seemed strange to Polk.

When the Major asked Ellspeth what he carried under a tarp in the wagon, the former Confederate captain explained that it was a Gatling gun captured from the blue bellies camped near the Del Carmens in the closing months of the war. The gun had since been hidden with other armament for the grand resumption of the Rebel cause below the Mexican border. When the dream never materialized, Ellspeth kept his hands on the Gatling gun.

'I'm going to teach these red bastards a lesson,' Ellspeth said, and the Major and the others said it was a good idea.

But a sudden rainstorm wiped out the tracks of the horsethieves. Disgruntled, they turned back and came suddenly upon a party of Kiowas on the move, looking half starved, sickly, and sullen. When they saw the white men they drew rein as if trying to decide whether to run or fight.

'Here's our horsethieves!' Ellspeth shouted, and whipped the tarp off the captured gun.

While the Kiowas watched from some fifty yards away, Polk and the Major helped lift the weapon out of the wagon. Only then did the Kiowas seem to realize their danger. One of them fired and Ellspeth fell dead into the mud.

There were about twenty Kiowas and they were herding no loose horses. As they milled about the Major leaped forward. With a firm hand he began to turn the crank of the gun, hurling sixty shots a minute out of the firing tubes.

It was over in a matter of seconds. No Kiowa or pony rose from the mud.

The Major and the others, a little shaken by what had taken place, decided it would be best not to mention the part the Gatling gun had played in the slaughter. He and Polk took the gun back to Hayfork and hid it in the barn. It remained there for some years until Darsie Polk could no longer stand the thought of its being practically at his fingertips. One night he took it from its hiding place, dug a large hole, and buried it.

The Major must have forgotten its existence. He never asked about it.

Later, the encounter between a handful of Texans and a war party of Kiowas became known as the Battle of Buffalo Creek. But to Darsie Polk it was murder. He felt as guilty as if he had been the one to turn the crank. He could have spoken up that day, protested. But he had kept silent.

Now the day was beginning to form up, yellow and strange-looking. A premonition of disaster deepened in the foreman. It was the sort of tension-ridden dawn that you could feel. The kind that caused old hatreds to explode into a killing; caused cattle to suddenly take it into their heads to run. A loco sort of day, for sure.

The last of 1885, and good riddance.

Polk rode out to Karns' wagon. He was sure the day would get nothing but worse, when he found Pete Shagrue lying on the ground. At first the rider he had sent to guard the outfit gave the appearance of death. But then Polk saw the overturned jug by one of Shagrue's outstretched arms.

With an oath, Polk dismounted and shook the man awake. 'Hell of a guard you are,' the foreman snarled. 'Getting yourself liquored up.'

Shagrue managed to get to his feet. Suddenly he leaned against a wheel of the wagon and vomited. 'Rot gut,' he groaned, and waved a hand at the wagon.

Frowning, Polk saw where Shagrue had

pulled aside the tarp to dig into the cargo. Polk whipped the tarp toward the rear of the wagon. The cargo that had so concerned Karns last night consisted of barrels and kegs and numerous stone jugs.

'A goddam whisky peddler,' Darsie Polk snorted. He stomped back to where Shagrue had been sick again.

'Rot gut,' Shagrue mumbled again. 'Jeez, I never drank such stuff.'

'Get your shirttail in your pants and come back to camp. Don't say anything to Justin about this. He's already got enough troubles.'

Shagrue washed his face in a stream that had ditched its way across the road. He and Polk rode back to camp.

Jethro Karns, wearing his coat with the yellow stripes, was drinking coffee. When he saw Shagrue's blood-shot eyes and slack features, he shot a suspicious glance in the direction of the wagon and the team of mules.

'Karns,' Darsie Polk said coldly, 'the minute we get that herd across the road you take your outfit and clear out. Take that girl with you.'

At that moment the yellowish haze that curtained the land spouted moisture. It was really more of a mist than a rain, but thick and penetrating. Thunder rumbled in the distance.

Justin came down the slant from the wagon, buckling on his gun. The brim of his hat was already soaked.

'Everybody hit leather,' he ordered. 'A jag of

lightning could set those cows to running!'

As they reached the herd, the morning turned sharply colder. Justin shouted orders to head the cows into the wind. It took some twenty minutes to get them on the move and to round up strays.

When this was done, Justin sent Shagrue and two of the men back to camp to get the wagons and the two women. Justin did not draw an easy breath until his Hayfork men had the last cow pushed north of the road. Above the howl of the gathering storm he saw a movement to his right. Turning in the saddle, he saw Jethro Karns whipping up his team of mules. The outfit was coming along the road directly toward them.

Justin shouted, 'Damn it, Darsie, why didn't you keep an eye on him!'

Wheeling his horse, Justin spurred toward the approaching wagon. The mount he had picked this morning was skittish, hard to handle. As Karns approached, Justin stood up in the stirrups, waving him back. He could hear the faint screech of wheels turning on dry axles.

But Karns didn't pull back; he kept coming. He was hunched over the reins, the tails of his striped coat whipping in the wind. The mules were lunging against their collars.

Angered by the man's stupid act, Justin drew his rifle and shouted, 'Hold up there or I'll shoot you off the seat!'

'Got to get this cargo to Princess Station!' Karns yelled. 'Blizzard coming, sure as hell!'

That was the last he spoke.

Justin never knew whether the mule team ran away or whether Karns panicked and used his whip. At that instant the wind increased. It came shrieking out of the north. The blast of frigid air sent the temperature tumbling. A gust of wind caught the tarp on Karns' wagon, lifted it high like a sail.

In the dimming light Justin snapped off a shot, but missed as his mount shied. And as he fought to get the animal under control he heard his brother's voice. Ford was shouting somewhere nearby into the fog of snow and rain.

'Samantha!' Ford was crying. 'Samantha!'

Justin froze in the saddle as he heard Ford shouting again. Realization that his brother was here, far up the trail, was so unsettling he let Karns and the wagon charge past him on the road. Another blast of wind whipped the tarp even higher, almost in the faces of a small pack of Hayfork cows cutting away from the main herd.

The flapping tarp so startled them they began to run. In an instant the terror was communicated to the rest of the animals. They began to wheel back the way they had come. Karns and the wagon headed directly into the path of the herd.

Karns saw his danger, stood up in the wagon

100

a moment, then leaped. First the mules were engulfed by the stampeding cattle, then the wagon. Karns huddled for a moment at the edge of the road. A steer bowled him over. Then the rest of them smashed him into the mud.

Spurring his horse, Justin kept to the fringe of the stampede, trying to reach Samantha's wagon. He shouted her name into the icy wind, even as Ford had done a few moments before. As the horse took the bit in its teeth, Justin saw that the fog of snow had thickened, a solid wall of white before his raging eyes.

With the ground shaking, he let the panicked horse pick its own path through the trees. Suddenly he was aware of an incline. It steepened. A ragged line of boulders appeared. Desperately he hauled in on the reins. The mad pace of the horse did not slacken. It tried to jump the line of boulders. Hoofs scraped rock. The horse squealed, lost its balance. Impact tore Justin from the saddle. Below he saw a long slope and more boulders in a sea of white at the bottom of a canyon.

He flipped in midair, hands wide to break his fall. He came down hard, rolled, felt a grinding blow at his temple. Then he solidly struck a shelf of rock. His momentum flung him into deep snow.

He lay stunned, while snow fell against his upturned face. 'Ford, I warned you not to follow her!' he shouted into the storm.

When he tried to move there was no feeling, no response in his limbs. Gradually he felt a warmth steal over his body. He tried to burrow deeper into the soft and comforting snow.

CHAPTER FOURTEEN

Ford Emery flung a forearm across his eyes to shield them against the driving snow. Almost obscured by the storm was the smashed hulk of a canvas-topped wagon. In a tangle of harness lay the team of mules, ground under the avalanche of cattle.

He'd seen stampedes in Texas, but never anything to equal this. That morning he'd lost his Appaloosa at Brightwater Creek. He was nearly across the creek when the animal's right foreleg broke through thin ice and became trapped in a pocket of boulders. The leg snapped like a stick. Ford was forced to shoot the animal.

Because he remembered landmarks from his last trip north in the spring, he angled for the Coldwell Road that he knew would take him to Princess Station.

As he hiked over the rough terrain, it started to drizzle. Then came snow. He wasn't too far from the road when, topping a rise, he came suddenly upon the Hayfork camp. He could see Samantha standing at the tailgate of a canvas-topped wagon, at the foot of a long slope.

He shouted her name and she turned, startled by the sound of his voice. A girl was with her, someone vaguely familiar. But he didn't stop to wonder about that. He began to run. Pete Shagrue, limping, was hitching up the team.

It was then that the ground began to shake. A numbing terror gripped Ford when he saw the tidal wave of cattle sweep through the trees. Saplings were uprooted, cows pinned and crushed against stouter trees by the pressure of other panicked animals. He screamed for Samantha to try and reach high ground, but nothing could be heard above the roar of the stampede. Already she was hurrying the girl up the slope. Shagrue tried to sprint around the wagon and also reach comparative safety. His bad leg slowed him. He was caught in the first wave.

As Ford scrambled up the slope, he turned to look back. Two Hayfork riders, trying to outrun the stampede, were swallowed up. He heard a piercing yell from Darsie Polk somewhere in the distance.

Out of the swirling snow came a rider. Obviously his horse was running away, and the rider seemed powerless to control it. Ford saw the animal racing straight up the slant, not ten feet away. Then horse and rider shot over a lip of boulders and disappeared.

And now it was over. Sounds of the herd were far to the south.

Ford was shaken. He held Samantha in his arms, felt her tremble. 'I'm sure it was Justin I saw,' Ford whispered. 'If he's alive, he'll freeze.'

'Oh, God, I pray that he is alive.'

Ivy Hollister staggered up. 'It was terrible, terrible,' she whimpered. 'Men and horses going down.'

'Samantha, you hang onto my belt,' Ford ordered. 'Miss, you hold tight to her hand. We're going down into that canyon. But we have to stay together.'

'I'm frightened,' Ivy said.

'We're all frightened,' Samantha told her. 'Hang onto my hand. All right, Ford, we're ready.'

In the driving snow they slowly made their way down the slope. They found Justin twenty feet above the canyon floor. Another five minutes and he would have been completely covered with snow. He would have frozen, and his body would probably not have been found until the spring thaw. Ford clawed away the snow. There was a gash at Justin's right temple. He was still alive, but that was about all. Justin had lost his hat, and his long hair was already stiff with ice.

'I'll have to carry him,' Ford said. He grunted and managed to sling Justin across his shoulders. The weight of him nearly caused

Ford's knees to buckle.

'Keep together,' Ford panted.

With Justin growing heavier at each step, Ford weaved his way down the canyon. Twice he was forced to rest before reaching the Coldwell Road. Down this road, he remembered, was Princess Station. He didn't even stop to calculate how far it might be. He just had to reach there.

Far in the distance was the sound of the herd, still running. They would run till winded, then push on, their instinct being to head away from a storm rather than into one.

Ford stumbled through a stand of iced cedars, his back bent with his burden. Drifting snow whipped his exposed face. He came to a striped cloak in the road and something meaty underneath.

Ivy screamed at the sight. He skirted the remains of a wagon, some dead mules and cattle. A pungent odor of whisky filled the air. Again he was forced to rest. Samantha insisted on helping carry Justin. Ford only shook his head.

'If we don't reach Princess Station, we're done,' he gasped. 'I've seen blizzards before, but this is the worst.'

The girl said, 'The station's down this road, I know. We'll find it. We've got to find it.'

They stumbled on again, the thickening snow giving a midnight dimness to the morning. At last they saw a lighted window through the gloom. In a few moments they came upon Princess Station, an oversized dugout with a sloping sod roof. Beyond was a barn, nearly obscured by the storm. Somehow Ford managed to get down a familiar flight of icy stairs. Samantha reached around him to hammer with her fist on the heavy locked door.

'Open up!' she cried. 'We need help!'

The door was unbolted and swung wide. Erdman Quine, holding a shotgun, stood in the opening.

'I thought I recognized your voice, Mrs. Quine,' he said. His gaze flicked to Ford. 'So you followed us. And I thought you had the nerve of a rabbit.'

The large room seemed deserted. A few Indian rugs were scattered about the floor. There were several puddles of muddy brown water. Four thick posts supported the ceiling. A short bar held dirty glasses and a half-empty bottle. Several small rooms opened off a rear corridor.

'No more stages through till the storm has passed,' Quine said pleasantly. 'Our little group will be quite alone.'

Ford had staggered to a wide bench against the wall. He carefully slid Justin off his shoulders to the bench, then sank to the floor, gasping for breath.

Samantha was on her knees beside Justin, rubbing his wrists, using a handkerchief on the wound at his temple. Putting the shotgun under one arm, Quine caught Samantha by her long hair. He pulled her back so that she fell across the floor. When she tried to spring to her feet and claw his face, he slapped her. The blow sent her reeling into one of the supporting timbers.

Tired as he was, Ford came up off the floor and dragged off a glove. He tried to reach the revolver under his coat. Hands seized his arms and he was rammed down into a chair. It was the first time he realized that Quine's two companions were also in the room. They stood on either side of the chair. Ford tried to get up, and Charlie Ivory hit him in the face. Ford fell back, his arms flopping. Ivy Hollister stood with hands pressed to her lips. Her face was dead white.

Samantha held out a hand of entreaty to Quine. 'Let me find bandages. Justin has a bad head wound.'

'He'll have a worse one.' His lips grinning under his rust-colored brush of mustache, Quine aimed the shotgun at Justin's head.

'No!' Samantha screamed, and flung herself between Quine and Justin, who lay still on the bench, his eyes closed.

Ivy said, 'I'll get cloth for bandages.' Her voice was reasonably steady. 'There's some in the back room,.'

'Watch her,' Quine snapped.

'Kelso Kane flicked a glance at Samantha.

'This is one blizzard I won't mind sittin' out.'

Quine shook his head. 'Charlie, get the horses out of the barn. Everybody else left this damned place on account of the storm. So will we.'

Kane gave him a long look. 'Hell of a day for ridin.'

'We head south,' Quine snapped. 'Soon as I kill Mr. Justin Emery.'

Samantha's knees seemed to sag; then she stiffened. Quine put out a hand to brush her aside, then took a quick appraisal. 'Muddy and damp, but still a handsome woman, Samantha.'

'Erd, I'll do anything. Don't kill him.' She bit her lips to stop their trembling. 'Murder will solve nothing.'

'Funny,' Quine said. 'We'd caught up with the Hayfork outfit, but I held off. I thought I'd wait and give myself a New Year's present tomorrow—by killing him.'

'Erd, please—'

'And then that damn herd stampeded so fast we almost got caught. Then we found this place, with everybody pulling out. And finally you show up. This is my lucky day.' Quine lifted the shotgun. 'Step aside, Samantha.'

She stood her ground. Ford lifted his head. 'Touch a woman and they'll hang you, Quine.'

'They tried to hang me once,' Quine said. 'Eh, Samantha? But not for touching a woman. They said I killed her lover.'

'He was not my lover.'

'And you haven't changed any.' Quine was thinned down, a stubble of rust-colored beard on his jaws. 'Playing brother against brother.'

'That isn't true.'

'Plead for his life, Samantha,' Quine said. 'Make it with tears, if you love him.'

'I love him very much.'

'Your trouble, Samantha, is that you love all men very much.' He jerked a thumb at Ivy. 'She was about your age when we married. You were also young and sweet, Samantha, before you found a certain delight in deceit.'

'You can't insult me, Erd.'

'Know what I thought about at Yuma? I'd remember the glow of your naked flesh in the lamplight.'

Samantha's face flamed.

Quine put the shotgun under his arm. His coat was mud-splattered, his heavy wool pants damp from the snow. 'Miss,' he said to Ivy, 'I'll give you fifteen minutes to get Emery conscious. It's better if he realizes who I am and why I am killing him.'

'I—I'll get bandages.' She turned, her coat open, her small boots tracking mud. She went into one of the rooms and in a moment returned with some clean white cloths.

'How come you know where things are around here?' Charlie Ivory demanded.

'I—I've been here before. With my aunt.'

Quine said, 'While she goes to work, I think

109

it only proper that you welcome me home, Samantha, in the manner of a wife eagerly accepting the return of her husband.'

'I won't do it, Erd.' Samantha's lips were white.

'Then I'll kill him now.' Stepping around her, he thumbed back the hammers of the shotgun.

Samantha moved swiftly and stood in front of the weapon, pushing her stomach against the twin barrels.

'Don't kill him. I'll do what you want.'

Ford managed to sit up straighter in his chair. 'My God, Samantha, you *can't*!' He tried to leap to his feet and drag up his revolver. But his belt was empty; he hadn't realized they had taken his gun.

Kelso Kane pushed him back into the chair. 'Set. Don't move.' Then Kane lifted his gaze to Samantha's back. She walked slowly toward one of the rooms, with Quine trailing her . . .

Ivy had put water on to heat. Kane and Ivory had gone over to the bar to drink whisky from the bottle left there. A man pounded on the door, begging to be let in. Charlie Ivory bellowed for him to go away.

Ford said, 'I'll help her carry the hot water.'

Ivory nodded. Kane didn't look around. He was watching the door Quine had closed behind him some minutes before.

When they got a pan of hot water to the floor beside the bench where Justin lay, Ford whispered, 'Is there a gun here, Ivy? A weapon of any kind?'

'No.'

'Where's Timmons, the man who used to run this place?'

'Cleared out, probably, like Quine said.' She was bathing Justin's temple wound. She looked around, her dark eyes staring. 'I didn't remember you at first. But I do now.'

'I was through here this spring.'

Ivy just looked at him.

'Your name didn't come to me,' Ford went on, 'till I saw you under this roof. I did some drinking here.'

'You talked to me all night about some girl and how you killed her. I thought you were crazy.'

'Listen, I'm going to try and get hold of a gun.'

'They'll shoot you.'

'I've got to try.' Ford listened to Justin's ragged breathing. Justin's eyes were closed.

'I know their kind,' Ivy said, nodding toward the pair at the bar. Her voice was tinged with despair. 'They'd kill you and laugh about it.'

'Help me distract them. I'll try and grab one of their guns.'

'It's no use.'

Charlie Ivory came over, tracking water from one of the puddles. 'Talk all you want, plan all you want. Won't do no good. When the time comes we'll do what we want.' He

111

gave Ivy a bold look. But she turned her back on him and started to bandage Justin's head.

At the bar, Kelso Kane drank and watched the closed door to the nearest bedroom. There was an oddly intent look to his slate-colored eyes.

CHAPTER FIFTEEN

Erd Quine put out a hand in the darkness of the room, feeling the shotgun at the edge of the bed. He wondered how many more minutes he could stand being shut up in the dugout. Not many. In some ways it reminded him of the 'hole' at Yuma. But this particular room held a bed and a woman. There was only rock at the special cell for incorrigibles at Yuma Prison; no bed, no woman.

He felt a drop of moisture on his cheek. Never was a sod roof that didn't leak. Again he felt a drop of water against his face.

What a contrast to the days at Yuma! There were times at Yuma, during the summer heat, when he would gladly have flung himself upon a floor like this and lapped up the puddles of muddy water like a thirst-crazy animal.

There had been times when he wanted the guards to kill him. Death was a kindness, weighed against the terrible waste of his natural life behind the rock walls of the prison.

He was not guilty of the crime they almost hanged him for; the crime they decreed should claim his life. But that didn't save him from death in a different way, the attrition of terrible years in the most merciless of prisons. Guilty, he might have been able to rationalize. The fact that he was innocent turned him at times into an animal.

Sometimes the guards beat him without reason, because he was a source of such constant trouble. At other times they were justified in beating him, for he made no secret of the fact that he would kill or maim if given the opportunity. Then let them hang him, and to hell with it.

He became one of the most hated men in the prison. Wagers were made among prisoners and guards as to the length of time he would be able to survive.

And then a man confessed that Ron McCallum owed him money and he had been the one to shoot McCallum in the back. When Quine heard the news at Yuma, he laughed in the face of the guard who brought him the message.

'I intended killing McCallum myself. This other boy just beat me to it. You see, McCallum was my wife's lover.'

The prison superintendent said it was a crime to set free upon society a man like Erdman Quine. But there was no legal way to hold him.

*   *   *

Quine flung out a hand, pressing his fingers into warm flesh. 'Your fault, Samantha. The whole thing was your fault.'

She gave a gasp of pain. 'You're hurting me.'

He removed his hand. 'How many times did you let McCallum make love to you?'

'Erd, I must go to Justin. Please.' She was sitting up in the bed, hair golden in the dim light, tumbling about her shoulders.

He saw the low ceiling, the walls. 'I've got to get out of this place.' He stood up. 'Get dressed, and don't try to get away.'

He went out to the front room, closing the door. Crossing to where Justin lay, he said, 'I might as well finish it. But I want her to watch.'

'Mr. Emery was kind to me,' Ivy said soberly. She had removed her coat. Her damp shirt clung to small breasts. 'Don't kill him. He's badly hurt.'

'Young lady, you're wasting breath begging for his life.'

'He has a big crew. They'll come looking for him. Have you ever thought of that?'

Quine gave her a hard smile. 'A lot of them got caught in the stampede. Last I saw, the ones still alive were chasing the herd. They'll never be able to turn those cows back into a storm like this.' He shook his head. 'They'll

114

keep going clear to Texas.'

Samantha, her face dead white, stepped from the room. Ignoring the way the others regarded her, she rushed to Justin's side and knelt beside the bench.

'Justin, Justin,' she whispered brokenly. Then she turned her head to look up at Quine. 'Your sort of vengeance was wasted on him. He's still unconscious. He'd have no idea of what was happening.'

Quine got her by an arm and pulled her up. 'Keep away from him.'

She stood, shaken. Ivory and Kane, their backs to the bar, watched her intently. She could feel the pounding of her heart. Any overt move, a harsh word, anything at all could result in chaos. She knew the symptoms well— the special way men looked at her. And now Quine had compounded the tension, the danger, by putting Justin's life on the block and then making her agree to degradation practically in front of these people.

When panic began to burgeon, she bit the knuckles of her clenched fist and tasted blood. The pain helped still her terror. Above all, she must save Justin. Nothing else mattered.

Quine dropped his hand from her arm and again tightened his grip on the shotgun. She glanced at Justin on the bench, his face so white, so still. Then she looked around and found Ford staring at her.

'Don't hate me, Ford.' She lifted a hand and

let it fall.

Erd Quine leaned over Justin. 'Why doesn't he wake up?'

A gust of wind rattled the narrow, snow-packed windows. One of the timbers creaked. The two men at the bar shifted their feet and glanced apprehensively at the ceiling, as if worried that it might collapse under the weight of the snow.

'Storm's getting worse,' Quine murmured.

Ford stood with his back to the wall. The nose Justin had broken in the fight at Hayfork gave him a tougher, more mature look, destroying his boyishness. 'When he said you were married to him once,' Ford said, 'I didn't believe it. I thought he was just some crazy fool wanting to make trouble for you and Justin.'

'Ford, I heard he was searching for me. I wanted to ask your advice that day. It's why I asked you to meet me by the barn.'

'Yeah, I should have known it was something like that.' Ford's lips tightened. 'I guess I've had a hell of a long ride for nothing.'

'Ford, you'll only make things worse,' Samantha said, glancing at Quine. Quine still stared down at Justin.

'And the first time he snaps his fingers,' Ford went on, his voice shaking, 'you run with him into the bedroom.'

Her eyes swung to his taut face, trying to impart a message: Can't you understand? I'm

116

trying to keep Justin alive! In any way at all, I'm trying to keep him alive!

Quine seemed thoughtful. 'We could make it back to Mexia Springs, get fresh horses, and push south out of this goddam storm.'

'We could set it out here,' Charlie Ivory said, glancing at Ivy.

'I think I'll shoot Emery and be done with it,' Quine said, and Ford tried to rush him. But Charlie Ivory put out his foot. Ford stumbled. As he fell, Kelso Kane struck him across the back of the head with the bottle. The remaining whisky showered over the dirty floor.

'You wasted good whisky,' Ivory said.

'There'll be more, in a place like this,' Kane said. 'There always is.'

Samantha drew a deep breath, knowing her moment of decision had come. In the back room she had appealed to Quine and he had ignored her. There had to be another way.

'Erd, now that you've found me again, why don't you take me out of here?'

Quine gave her a tight smile. 'You're no actress. Don't try to be one.' He put his attention back on Justin as if willing him to regain consciousness.

'I'll go away with you, if that's what you want,' Samantha said.

'You know damn well it's what you're going to do.'

'But I'll go willingly. There is a difference.'

117

She met his hazel eyes. 'A great deal of difference, Erd.'

Quine's glance flicked to Justin. 'You're making a bargain?'

'Justin's life.'

Quine leaned over Justin, listened to his heavy breathing. 'I don't think he'll live anyway. What's the difference whether I kill him or he just dies?'

'The difference is this, Erd.' Samantha's hands were clenched at her sides. 'I once held a great warmth and affection for you. A generous act such as this could help restore it.'

Quine stood with the shotgun under one arm, rubbing the stubble on his jaw. 'I think you lied about divorcing me.'

'Papers were sent to you at Yuma. Erd, you know I'm not lying.'

A faint smile stirred the ends of his mustache. 'Justin Emery of Hayfork ranches, dead of natural causes,' he mused. 'That's the correct way to put it, I believe. And you, his grieving widow. Yes, I guess at last I recognize the fact that you did divorce me. At the proper time, however, remarriage will be in order.'

'Whatever you want, Erd.'

'However, if he doesn't die I'll kill him. You know I speak the truth.'

'Yes, I know you do.'

'First stop Mexia Springs,' Quine said.

Kelso Kane looked unhappy, but Charlie Ivory said, 'Erd, we can use an extra girl.' He

118

stepped toward Ivy.

But Quine shook his head. 'She stays. One woman to watch is enough.'

When coats were buttoned or belted or laced against the storm, Quine stepped over the prostrate Ford and opened the door. He let Ivory and Kane go first, then Samantha. She put her head down, the fierce wind whipping the ends of the scarf she had tied over her hair.

In the barn they got the horses and rode south, the blizzard at their backs.

'I feel better,' Quine said. 'Even in the storm, I feel better. In there I felt like I was caged.'

'Storm won't last more than another day,' Ivory said. 'It'll blow itself out.'

'I got a feeling about this one,' Kelso Kane said, his voice muffled by the turned-up collar of his blanket coat.

Samantha wept, the tears freezing to her cheeks. Whether the storm trapped and killed them was unimportant. She was already dead. The actual warm lethargy that preceded freezing to death would be preferable to this, the silent death she would have to endure with Erd Quine.

CHAPTER SIXTEEN

The storm did not blow itself out. Everywhere through the murk Samantha could see cattle drifting south. Occasionally riders, scarves across their faces, their brows bleached white with ice, trailed the cows, making no attempt to turn them back into the storm. Cattle by the thousands drifted down from the north; they got into what was later termed their 'blizzard gait.' And there was no stopping them. In normal times a cow would either charge or ignore a man afoot. A man in the saddle was something else again, and could usually control them. But on this last day of 1885 the cattle put their rumps to the blizzard and kept going south. If a horseman didn't get out of the way he was trampled.

Near the outskirts of Mexia Springs they came upon a team and wagon. In the wagon were a man and a woman wrapped in a blanket, frozen to death. The team had broken through well-planks and half fallen into the well.

Finally they reached Hearn's Store. Quine ordered Ivory to take the horses to shelter. Some dozen men lounged about the store and bar, some in chairs, their faces whipped raw by the storm, their eyes mirroring exhaustion.

A silence fell upon them when they saw

Samantha.

Quine, the shotgun with the sawed barrels held under his heavy coat, took Samantha by an arm and pushed her to the counter. 'Hearn, I want a room where my woman and I can get sleep for the night,' Quine told the man wearing overalls.

Hearn nodded. 'Who can sleep on a night like this?'

'Or who could think of sleep with a woman like that,' a man said, somewhere beyond the large stove in the center of the room.

Quine turned, trying to identify the speaker in the dimly lighted room. 'Don't make the mistake of repeating that remark, whoever you are.'

Something in Quine's voice caused the men around the stove to stiffen. They eyed the shotgun he held carelessly now under his arm.

Samantha was brushing snow from her hair when she saw Darsie Polk across the room. The Hayfork foreman was sprawled in an armchair near the stove. His right leg, resting on a bench, was splinted and bound with torn strips of dirty underwear. His eyes seemed sunken into his thinned face. The ragged beard was no longer gray, but dead white.

'Where's Justin?' he demanded thinly.

Quine turned quickly. 'Who's that?'

Samantha explained, 'Justin's foreman.'

The pressure of Quine's fingers on her arm caused her to break off. Quine leaned close.

121

'Don't tell him where Justin Emery can be found. If you do—' he pointed significantly at the shotgun—'I'll backtrack and finish him.'

Samantha swallowed, made an appealing gesture to the Hayfork foreman across the room. 'Justin must be with the herd.'

'Every man still able to set a saddle is far south by now,' Polk said. 'I don't think Justin's with 'em.'

'Then he may be lost in the storm,' Samantha said.

Polk's lips thinned. 'You didn't waste time grieving, did you?' His gaze swung to Quine, who stood at her elbow.

'Your mouth, old man,' Quine said, 'keep it shut.'

Charlie Ivory came in, whipping his arms across his chest to warm them. Everyone turned to stare at the big man. He joined Kane at the bar. Kane had helped himself to a bottle. He drank from it, the narrowed eyes in the long brown face studying Samantha.

'Erd, I was born under a dark star,' Kane said, lowering the bottle. 'I never have luck with cards or women. How come some hombres have it all?'

'You call this storm luck?'

'You know the kind of luck I mean,' Kane said softly.

Quine gave him a hard smile. 'I'm going to my room. If you boys hear anything that I should know, come and wake me.'

122

Hearn led the way down a narrow corridor and set a lamp on a table. The room was small, with only a cot.

Several times during the night Samantha tried to get away. Each time Quine awakened. Then she would lie in the darkness, her heart pounding. Wind whipped the walls, whistled through cracks in the timbers. The building shook. Even under the pile of stinking blankets and robes her feet were freezing. Finally Quine warmed her feet with his, but it gave her no comfort.

Even at dawn, which was barely distinguishable from night, she had no chance. She dressed hurriedly, but Quine left the room first, ordering her not to try to get away. He repeated his warning of the night before. He could return to Princess Station—and she knew damn well what that meant. All she had wanted was to get word in some way to Darsie Polk that Justin needed help.

The store was nearly deserted when Quine told her to come out front. Men had drifted during the night, somebody said, trying to beat the storm. Darsie Polk still sat in his chair, his eyes bright with fever.

For breakfast she stood at the counter and drank strong coffee and munched a cold biscuit. Quine dickered with Hearn for fresh horses.

When he sent Ivory and Kane into the storm to saddle the horses at the barn,

Samantha moved over to the stove to warm her hands. 'Darsie, listen to me,' she whispered, bending down as if the heel of her boot needed attention.

The Hayfork foreman said, 'Slut,' through his teeth.

She straightened up, her face losing color. Her one chance was gone. Quine came to take her arm.

'Let's be on our way,' Quine said.

Everywhere that day they came upon dead cattle and horses.

'Kee-ryst!' shouted Charlie Ivory, above the roar of the blizzard. 'Won't it never let up?'

'The goddam end of the world, that's what,' muttered Kelso Kane. He twisted his hunched body in the saddle to stare at Samantha. 'A man should take what he wants, at a time like this.'

'You try it,' Quine said, swinging close. 'It will be the end of the world for you, for sure.'

CHAPTER SEVENTEEN

For three days Ford Emery drank steadily from the stone jugs at Princess Station. Self-preservation kept him sober enough to stagger out for more firewood. He exhausted a pile of logs near the dugout, then began tearing apart the barn. In a root cellar under the east wall,

Ivy found a side of beef left to hang. With an axe, Ford chopped off enough of the frozen meat for their meals. Ivy cooked it over the wood stove in the center of the room.

During this time Justin moved the fingers of his right hand, then his arm. He rolled his eyes and stared across the room at his brother. Ford and Ivy had moved him to a bed dragged in from a back room, so he would be close to the stove.

Ford's head ached from the bottle smashed against his skull. He felt like an old, old man. Then Justin uttered his first sound and it so startled Ford that he turned suddenly, spilling whisky across his shirt.

Justin glared at Ford. His voice lashed out with a trace of its old vigor. 'You son of a bitch, get out of my sight!'

Ford went white. With his bloodshot eyes and smashed nose he little resembled the handsome Ford Emery of the Midpoint place. 'Justin, what you called me reflects on our mother—'

'She didn't give birth to you. She couldn't. I don't know where you came from and I don't care—' Justin's strength ran out and he gripped the edges of the straw mattress with his shaking hands. 'Just get out of my sight. Clear out.' His voice faded and he closed his eyes.

'I'm not leaving,' Ford said. 'With nobody to feed the stove you'd freeze to death.'

'Who gives a damn?' Justin said, clenching his teeth.

'I care,' Ivy said quietly, and smiled down at him.

Justin opened his eyes and stared at her. He didn't speak, only nodded his head that he understood.

Inside a week Justin could hobble about the room. 'Something was pinched in my back. I landed on it when I fell. It still aches, but I have feeling.'

'I'm so thankful,' Ivy said, beaming up at him. 'You're gaining strength. I can really care for you now.'

'I remember the horse going crazy and throwing me. But how did I get here?'

Before Ivy could answer Ford said, 'Harvey Timmons runs this place. He packed you here, then went on his way.'

'Seems that I am in his debt,' Justin muttered.

Later Ivy gave Ford a strange look. 'Why didn't you tell Justin the truth?'

'Maybe he wouldn't believe it,' Ford said bitterly. 'Even if he did, it's something he wouldn't want to believe.' He gave her a look. 'Don't tell him different, understand?'

'You trying to be a martyr or something?'

Ford shook his head. 'I've learned that it's easier to tell people what they want to believe. They're happier, and so are you.'

Several times men pounded on the door,

demanding admittance. But Ford refused to unbar the door. He had no weapon of any kind, no way to defend women.

When he went out for wood he would carefully scout the area before leaving the dugout.

One day when he returned from the frozen outside world he was surprised to see Justin on his feet. 'I'm glad to see you're up,' Ford said, and filled the woodbox.

'Don't wait around for me to completely regain my strength,' Justin said coldly. 'Not if you're wise, you won't.'

'Justin, you don't understand.'

'That's the way you explain everything.' Justin's lips twisted. 'People just don't understand. I told you to stay in Texas, not to try and follow Samantha.'

'I followed for a reason.'

'That I damn well know.' The talk weakened Justin. Ivy helped him lie back on the bed.

Her accusing gaze swung to Ford. 'Why don't you quit trying to argue with him?'

The next day the storm lifted a little more. Sun briefly touched the east windows, then was lost in the familiar yellow murk.

Ford tore off planks from a corn crib and cut them into stove lengths. He carried these to the dugout. When he approached the door he heard Ivy say, 'Justin, you could sell out. In Arizona we could get a new start. Both of us.'

'We'll see,' Justin muttered.

Ford spent the rest of the afternoon on a pair of snowshoes he had found in a back room. Everywhere he found dead cows and horses. Two miles from the station he came upon a camp. Three cowhands, whipped by the storm, were gathered about a small fire.

'Every damn cow south of the Canadian line has headed for Texas,' one of the men said in answer to Ford's question about range conditions.

'Only one cow in ten made it,' another put in. 'The rest froze stiff.'

'Have you come upon any Hayfork men?'

'Nope, but a fella comin' nawth yesterday said he seen more dead Hayfork cows 'tween here an' Mexia Springs than a man could count.'

'I hear the banks are already gettin' worried,' the first man said. 'We tried to save all the cows we could for our boss. There ain't much to save. All we can do is keep pushin' south.'

When Ford returned to the dugout he found Justin asleep. He got Ivy by an arm and forced her into a back room. 'I overheard you talking about Arizona,' he said.

She shrugged. She had found a wool dress. It was too large, but she had belted it so the hem wouldn't drag. 'I like the sound of Arizona.'

'As for him selling out, maybe there won't

be anything left to sell.'

Her dark eyes were defiant. 'I think you'd better leave here. He's getting stronger. He talks against you.'

'You have no right to go on with him this way. At least tell him about yourself.'

'Maybe he loves me. What's so wrong for me to want a chance in life?'

'He told you he's in love with you?'

'A man doesn't have to say those things out loud. There are other ways he lets you know.'

'When I was out getting wood, probably.'

'When you were gone today.' She looked away. 'Very much he showed me that he loves me.'

'I see.'

'He's been hurt and he needs me.'

'You need his money. The money you think he has.'

'You go ahead and tell him what you want. He wouldn't believe you no matter what you say. And you never saw me before in your whole life. Unless it was the times I came here with my aunt—' Her voice broke. With the tips of her fingers she wiped her eyes.

'You're not very concerned about your aunt in this blizzard.'

Ivy turned for the door and stood for a moment, her shoulders slumped. 'Why pretend? I don't have an aunt. I don't have anybody. Sometimes I wish I'd never been born.'

'We all wish that at one time or another.' Ford gave a small laugh. 'Lord knows the world hasn't been any brighter with me in it.'

She looked around, surprised. 'Strange that you should put it that way. I've said the same thing—about myself.'

CHAPTER EIGHTEEN

When the roads were fairly clear, Darsie Polk was able to hire a wagon and have a man drive him up from Mexia Springs. His broken leg still had not healed. The splints were like barbs pressed against nerve ends. When he came to the scene of the stampede he had the driver haul up. Here and there he could see a hoof or a horn sticking out of the deep snow. He could see remnants of smashed wagons. A chest of drawers lay splintered under a rock overhang, and near it lay a woman's bright red scarf.

'Red becomes her,' Darsie Polk said through his teeth.

'What'd you say?' asked the driver.

'Nothing. Let's try and get through to Princess Station. Maybe, just maybe—'

Ford was shoveling snow off the steps of the large dugout when the wagon appeared. He put aside the shovel and shook hands with the old man.

'Justin's inside,' Ford said, and explained how Justin had been unable to move after the fall into the canyon. But now he seemed to be getting about.

'Saw Samantha,' Polk said.

'With Erd Quine?'

'With a man. Three men, really. Didn't take her long to quit Justin, now did it?'

'I've had a chance to think things out. She did it to save Justin's life.'

Polk gave him a hard smile. 'I used to tell myself that I was wrong about her. That her comin' into Justin's life was good. Funny how a man tries to lie to himself.'

'Don't condemn her, Darsie. I can use the loan of a gun if you have an extra.'

Polk gestured toward a rifle wrapped in a blanket lying on the floorboards of the wagon. 'Help yourself.'

The driver and Ford carried Polk into the station. Justin shook the foreman's hand and clapped a hand to his shoulder, but he did not smile.

'You better come home, Justin,' Polk said, darting a glance at the dark-haired Ivy. 'Things are in bad shape.'

'Home is up north. At Ketcher.'

'After a storm like that,' Polk advised, 'a man should head south for a spell.'

Ford said, 'That agreement we signed means nothing, Justin. You belong at Midpoint.'

131

Justin rubbed at the beard on his jaws. He had not shaved since two days before the stampede. 'Darsie, you see any of the boys?'

Polk shook his head. 'If any of 'em lived through the stampede they're in Texas by now.' His angry gaze centered on Ivy. 'It was that whisky peddler *uncle* of yours that started them cows running.'

'Leave her alone,' Justin snapped. 'Head south and see if you can find any Hayfork cows.' He jerked a thumb at Ford. 'And take him with you!'

'What you aim to do, Justin?' Darsie Polk asked quietly.

'Think and get my strength back. For now, that's what I aim to do.' He added, 'Darsie, I'm sorry about your leg.'

'Could just as easy have been my head. I'm lucky, I reckon.' He stood on his good leg, the driver and Ford supporting him by the arms. 'I saw your wife, Justin.'

Justin's face closed. 'Never mind that,' he said.

'She's not his wife,' Ivy said, coming to stand at Justin's side. 'Not now she isn't.'

'You already got the Hayfork brand on this one, Justin?' Polk said, inclining his head at Ivy.

'Darsie, I gave you a job to do. Get Ford out of my sight. That's the biggest favor you can do for me.'

When they had gone and Justin was alone in

the dugout with Ivy, she cooked him some supper—nearly the last of the frozen beef from the root cellar.

When they had finished she said, 'Justin, the roads are open now. Can't we leave?'

'Not yet.'

'People will start to come through here and—'

'You afraid of people?'

A flush touched her cheeks. 'I'd like us to go to Arizona. We talked about it.'

'I know. But I have to settle some business first.'

She turned, clasping his rough frostbitten hands in hers. 'Surely you have a lawyer. Let him handle your affairs.'

It wasn't the kind of business he meant. 'For a girl, you seem to know a lot about business,' he said with an indulgent smile.

'I hear talk. You know.' She made an expansive gesture that lifted her small breasts under the wool dress. 'Friends are always dropping in at my aunt's—'

'You have no folks except your aunt?'

'I have you, Justin. The good Lord sent me you.'

'A squeaky wagon brought us together. A wagon and your Uncle Jethro,' he added.

'You didn't like him, and I don't blame you. But I'm sorry he's dead . . . Justin, can't we leave here? You can hire a wagon and some men and—'

'Just give me time, Ivy. A little more time.' He patted her arm. 'I feel stronger today. Maybe you can help me move the bed back into that room.'

'I—I don't like that room, Justin.'

He looked at her. 'What's liking or disliking a room got to do with it? It's just a place to sleep.'

'I don't like it, Justin,' she persisted.

'Better to sleep back there than out here. As you said yourself, people are starting to move about. Any time we might have visitors.'

That afternoon he moved the bed back into the room, taking his time, sitting down when overcome with weariness. That night Ivy seemed tensed up, afraid.

In the morning she combed her dark hair and looked at him. 'You haven't said one word about that woman.'

'You mean Samantha?'

'I even hate the sound of her name.'

'Why?'

'Because of the terrible things she's done to you. Being married before and telling you she was a widow. And with her husband in prison because he lost his head with jealousy and decided to kill her lover. Only he didn't kill him. Another man did before Quine got the chance, and this man finally confessed and—'

'Ivy, I've heard most of it.'

'You were unconscious. How could you?'

'The body failed to respond, but the brain

134

still lived. It's there in my mind, all a jumble now. It'll take tune to sort things out.'

'She was bad even before she married you. Married to Quine, and she still had a lover.'

'I don't recall the details. That part is fuzzy. She denied this, of course—the part about having a lover?'

'What woman wouldn't deny it?'

'When I feel able I'll probably go after Samantha.'

Ivy looked surprised, then hurt. 'You love her.'

'Somebody steals a horse,' Justin said, his voice low and bitter. 'Maybe you don't particularly like the horse or want it. But you go after the thief. It's a matter of principle.'

'I guess I wasted my time,' Ivy said in a small voice, 'trying to turn you against her. No matter what you say, you still love her.'

'One day everything will be straight in my mind again. Then we'll see.' He took a deep breath. The wound on his temple had healed, but it would leave a scar. 'First I've got to start putting things back together.' He gave a small laugh. 'If only I had a ring like Edgar's.'

'Who's Edgar?'

'A lawyer who had more brains than the rest of us. His ring is probably the only damn thing left in the cow country that's worth more than two dollars. He sold out most of his cattle holdings last year.'

'It was a bad storm, sure,' Ivy said in a small,

hopeful voice. 'But every winter there are storms and you cowmen survive.'

'Only every century is there a storm like this.'

He started taking walks. He made it to the barn and back on the first day, using the snowshoes Ford had left behind. On the second day he walked around the barn. Each day he increased the distance a quarter of a mile.

One day when he was gone, Harvey Timmons, astride a work horse, arrived at the station. He came in, blowing out his frosty breath, waddling in his heavy clothes.

His fat face beamed when he saw Ivy at the bar. 'I figured you and Jethro was lost out somewheres in the storm.'

'I was afraid of this,' Ivy said in a dull voice. 'That you'd come back before we left.'

Timmons stripped off his gloves and looked at her in surprise. 'Why shouldn't I come back? Run the station here, don't I? Hell, this may be our last year here, Ivy. I hear the steam cars will be comin' through before too long. Stage lines are done, I reckon.' His thick lips sucked mournfully as he added, 'Most everything is done. Cowmen busted, so I hear—'

'Harvey, listen to me.' Ivy hurried to the stove where he was warming his hands.

'I never got more'n ten mile east of here the first day of the big blow. I swore I wasn't goin' to get penned up here for another winter. And here I am back.' He gave her a crooked grin. 'Damn near froze. Lord was with me, I reckon.'

'Justin Emery was hurt. He's been staying here.'

Timmons looked down at her small face. 'Glad you had company, Ivy.' He glanced around the big empty room with its puddles of brown water on the floor. 'Where is that damn Jethro Karns, anyhow?'

'He—he was killed.'

Timmons stared; then a tight smile touched his lips. 'Did you wait till his back was turned to you, then shoot him through the blankets?'

'He caused a stampede. It crushed him to death.'

Timmons rubbed his hairy jaw. 'No great loss.'

'It was a squeaky wagon that caused it. Jethro had a good wagon, but he sold rot gut to some cowboys and they wrecked his wagon. He had to buy another one, and get more whisky— He was a damn fool.'

'Now that he's dead, you can work for me direct. We got one more year, maybe, like I said. Then the railroad will come through.' He scowled. 'Hope to hell the cow business ain't hurt as bad as some claim. Without the cowhands comin' up the trail—'

'Harvey, I'm not making myself clear.' Ivy glanced anxiously at the closed door as if

137

expecting Justin to return at any moment. 'I'm in love with Justin Emery. *In love.*'

'Well, now, ain't that a bit unusual?'

'I hope to marry him,' she went on firmly. 'You do one thing to spoil it for me, Harvey—' Her voice began to shake. 'I swear to you that if you do, I'll—'

He stared at the tears spilling across her cheeks. 'Ivy, I don't figure to spoil things.' He patted her hand. 'I wish you well. But if I was you, I'd find new territory. Around here folks got long memories.'

'I'm trying to convince Justin we should go to Arizona.'

Timmons laughed. 'Funny, but I never figured you for a *chica* with brains and gumption both—the way you used to let Jethro Karns keep you on a short rein.'

'I grew up on that short rein,' Ivy said bitterly. 'I didn't know any better. I'm glad it's over.'

'I hope it's over for you, Ivy, if that's what you want. I really do.'

'Listen, Harvey, there's something else. Justin thinks you saved his life.'

'Me? I never even met the man. How could I?'

'His brother wants it that way, and I guess he knows Justin better than I do. So Justin will probably thank you. You can shrug it off. You know how.'

When Justin returned, his face red from the

138

cold, Ivy introduced Timmons. 'He runs the place here, Justin,' Ivy explained. 'He—he's a friend of my aunt's. He helped her settle out west of here.'

Justin shook Timmons' hand. 'You're the one saved my neck in the storm.'

'Well, I—'

'Harvey's modest,' Ivy said quickly, 'He doesn't like to remember that he's the one packed you in from the canyon.'

Timmons seemed anxious to change the subject. 'I been eatin' horse meat for three days. There's a cow froze stiff as a barn wall out yonder. We'll have steaks for supper.'

CHAPTER NINETEEN

Because of the weather, Justin decided to return to Midpoint. Ford would just have to put up with him until the tangle got unsnarled. When he reached Texas he was saddened to learn that Smitty had been one of those lost in the stampede. Ford had asked his widow to come out to Hayfork and cook for the men.

At the Midpoint place Justin received more bad news. Edgar Dobbs drove out from town. The lawyer had lost weight and Justin noticed that the diamond ring was missing.

On the veranda, they went through a throat-clearing awkwardness. 'Is Samantha enjoying her stay in St. Louis?' Dobbs asked.

'Yes. The storm was quite a shock,' Justin said. 'It's good for her to be among old friends.'

'Maude and the girls are on their way home from Yurrope. Guess they saw most of it anyhow. Maude likes Italy the best, so she wrote.'

Justin was silent for a moment. 'You were smart to clear out of the cow business, Edgar.'

'A real cowman never gets out. Not clear out.' Dobbs gave Justin a small tight smile. They were sitting in tipped-back chairs. 'I used my money to buy shares in the RB outfit.'

'But I hear they're broke,' Justin exclaimed in surprise.

'I know,' Dobbs said with a sad shake of his head. They sat in silence for a moment on the veranda. Below the railing Justin could see the remains of Samantha's bed of flowers. Something twisted in him. Gradually, these past days, the fog and confusion in his mind had been clearing.

Edgar Dobbs gave a long sigh. 'Reckon I got some bad news. RB isn't the only outfit bust. You asked me to find out how things stood up at Ketcher.'

'And the bank's already got it,' Justin guessed.

'How'd you know that?'

Justin spread his hands. 'We raised cows on paper grass furnished by the bank. Now it's

140

bitter grass.'

'Sad, sad days,' Dobbs agreed dolefully. 'Last year this time I had me close to half a million dollars in cash.' He turned to Justin. 'Why ain't a man ever satisfied?'

Justin was leaning forward in his chair. He stared down at the dead stalks, the weeds in the plot of ground below the porch. The twisting under his heart grew to a pain.

'You sick, Justin?' Dobbs said in alarm.

'Just a twitch of pain. Takes a long time to recover.'

'Must have been some fall you had.'

'Horse went crazy. Stampedes can do that. The horse must have been cold-jawed and I didn't know it. When I tried to haul it in, it just kept going.' Justin shivered. 'Right over the edge of that cliff.'

'Wonder you weren't clear buried in snow. Lucky there was enough of you sticking out of the snow for Ford to see.'

Justin turned in his chair. 'What do you mean by that, Edgar?'

The sharpness of Justin's tone caused the lawyer to lose color. 'Why—why, he's the one who located you.'

'Ford told you that?'

'Ford never said anything about it.'

'Then how in the hell—'

Dobbs squirmed in his chair. 'Didn't intend for it to slip out. I might've known I could never keep anything from an Emery.'

141

'Go on, Edgar.'

'Letter came for Mrs. Dobbs. I—well, I opened it because I knew Maude wouldn't be home for a spell. It was from Samantha!'

'Samantha!'

Dobbs nodded. 'I don't usually open my wife's mail, but—'

'What did Samantha say?' Justin's fingers were clamped around the lawyer's wrist.

'She just said she wanted Maude to know that Ford did a fine thing, saving your life. She wanted the whole town to know it.' Dobbs gave a small shrug. 'Reckon Samantha knows that giving Maude news to spread is more efficient than the telegraph.'

'What else did she say?'

'Justin—' Dobbs winced and tried to pry Justin's fingers from his wrist. 'You got your strength back, that's for sure. You like to bust my bones?'

Justin removed his hand. 'I'm sorry, Edgar.' Although the day was cool, he drew a bandana from his pocket and wiped his forehead. 'Is that all Samantha wrote?'

'That's all. She just said Ford never had many people to speak out for him.'

'Didn't she mention my name?'

'Nope. She had no reason to, seeing as how she probably writes you regular anyhow. Reckon she forgot Maude was in Yurrope with the girls.'

'You still have the letter?'

'Reckon.'

'And the envelope?'

'Can't rightly remember about that.'

'You notice the postmark?'

'Well, come to think of it, the postmark was from somewhere in New Mexico. Funny but, looking back on it, that's one of the reasons I opened the letter. I wondered who in New Mexico would be writing Maude. Thought it might be some of her kinfolk maybe gone out that way and were sick or something.'

'Do you remember where in New Mexico?'

'That I don't, Justin.'

'Try and find that envelope, Edgar. I'll appreciate it mightily.'

Dobbs turned and looked up into Justin's tight face. 'Has Samantha left you?' he asked quietly.

'She's in St. Louis, Edgar. St. Louis—Oh, why try and pretend?'

'The minute I read the letter and saw she didn't mention you I figured she'd left you. I didn't want to say anything about it unless you wanted to tell me.' Dobbs sighed. 'But I had to go and open my big mouth about Ford. It's what I meant when I said I should know better than to try and keep anything from an Emery.'

'It doesn't matter now.'

'If you want to pretend she's in St. Louis, I'll play your game. If anybody asks,' he went on, holding Justin's eye, 'I'll say she's in St. Louis like you claim.'

143

'Just try and find the envelope. I'll be in town in a day or so.' Justin smiled.

'For a man who's had bad news about the Ketcher place, you seem almighty pleased about something.'

'Edgar, keep the letter to yourself, will you?'

'I've only told it around town that Ford saved your neck. I never said where I heard it.'

'Tell me, did anyone believe it? About Ford?'

'Well, all I can say is that there seemed to be considerable skepticism in the air.'

They went down the veranda steps to where Dobbs' buggy and team were, on the east side of the house. Esther Smith, a spare, gray-haired woman, was hanging out wash on a line. She gave Dobbs a brief nod and he tipped his hat. She entered the house by the back door.

'Smitty was a good man,' Justin said soberly. 'I feel responsible for his death.'

'Don't hold it against yourself, Justin.' Dobbs untied his team from a stump. 'This is a business fraught with danger, as the man said.'

Justin shrugged. Smitty's widow came to a window and drew a curtain to let in more sunlight. Ford had partially furnished the house with second-hand pieces purchased in Midpoint, but he still occupied his lean-to. Since his return, Justin had shared the bunkhouse with the men. But occasionally he would come up to the house and sit on the veranda. He would stare across the flats and

144

ponder his future. He knew what he was going to do, but he wanted to be a whole man again when he started out.

'Justin, what do you aim to do about the cow business?' Dobbs asked.

'We're skinning dead cows, Edgar. This year we'll sell hides. It's about all we have to sell. Or rather all Ford has to sell.'

At that moment Ivy Hollister appeared from the opposite side of the house. When she saw Dobbs and Justin standing together, she flushed and hurried back the way she had come.

'Must be shy,' Dobbs observed. 'She was in town the other day with Ford. Ford tells it that she's some sort of kinfolk.'

'I suppose you might say she's been close to the Emerys.'

'Mighty pretty little thing, dressed up as she was the other day.' Dobbs glanced at the sky. 'If the clouds had only brought rain last summer and fall, instead of all that cussed snow this winter, we'd be some rich, wouldn't we, Justin?'

Justin made no reply. From where he stood he could see a portion of the south wall of the barn across the yard.

When Dobbs drove off, Justin walked down to the barn. There he halted, looking at the frozen ground that still bore bootmarks from the day he had fought his brother. Justin was still standing there when Ford came riding around a corner of the barn. Seeing Justin surprised him. Ford reined in, sitting his saddle uneasily.

'Step down, Ford,' Justin said.

Ford dismounted and let the rein ends settle to the ground. Justin nodded at the gun rig strapped to his brother's waist. 'You've taken to wearing a revolver. It's out of style these days.'

'I was caught out once without one. A man threatened to use a knife on me. I never forgot it.'

'Oh,' Justin said, and slid a hand along his jaw, then upward to feel the scar at his temple. 'I thought you carried a gun because of me. That you were afraid I'd try and beat you up again.'

'I'm not afraid of you, Justin,' Ford said quietly. 'I don't need a gun for you.'

Justin met Ford's gaze, then shoved his hands into the hip pockets of his canvas pants. His fleece-lined jacket hung open, baring his shirtfront to the feeble sunlight.

'That day here at the barn,' Justin said. 'Why would she ask you to meet her here?'

'Why do you care, after all this time?'

Justin closed his eyes. 'She could have asked you to meet her at the house,' he mused. 'I was to be gone all that day. Then that horse spooked and tried to jump the wire fence and—' He shook his head at the memory. 'No, she asked you to meet her here so it would be in the open. But out of sight of the house, of the bunkhouse. But very much in the open. A woman bent on seduction doesn't do it that way.'

'I figured you hated her!'

'Did she ever get a chance to tell you what she wanted that day?'

'You never gave her a chance to tell you, that's for sure.'

'I know that.'

'She was worried. She'd lied to you about Quine being dead. She thought he'd never get out of prison. She wanted to talk to you about it, but you had other things on your mind.'

Justin's smile was grim. 'Yes, I was going to be worth one million dollars by the time I was thirty.'

'Samantha wanted my advice. Then—' Ford's cheeks flushed.

'Then?' Justin prompted.

'She just stood there, so damn lovely I lost my head. I couldn't help myself. But it wasn't her doing. It was all mine. I tried to tell you that, but each time you knocked me down. God knows I tried to tell you.'

'God knows you did, Ford.' Justin stepped close. Ford stiffened as if awaiting Justin's fist, and ready to counter. But Justin only put a hand on his arm. 'Thanks for saving my life. I didn't know about it until today.'

'I'm surprised you found out. I'm further surprised that you gave much of a damn either

147

way.'

Ford picked up the reins and stalked away, leading his horse.

Later Ford found Ivy behind the house. He caught her by an arm and twisted her around to face him. 'Did you tell Justin I was the one packed him to Princess Station?'

'No, honest, Ford, I didn't say anything.'

'Then how did he find out?'

They stood quietly together for a moment. Then Ivy said, 'Ford, I enjoyed you taking me to town the other day. It was the first time I've seen a real town in a long while.'

'If Justin finds out he'll probably raise hell. But somehow I don't care whether he does or not.' Ford's face was suddenly suffused with anger. Ivy, thinking it was meant for her, gave a small cry of alarm.

But Ford ignored her. He returned to the barn. Justin was no longer standing there. He found Justin at the house, where Esther Smith was preparing supper. These days the men ate at the big table in the kitchen.

Ford saw Justin standing with his back to the door, running his hand over a stove lid. And Ford was reminded that once he had done this himself—after Samantha had gone north with Justin. Ford had come here one day in loneliness and touched the metal surface of something that had meant a great deal to her. The range had not been moved north with the rest of the furniture. Ford remembered

Samantha's face the day Justin had the range delivered from town in the big wagon.

Justin heard Ford speak his name. He turned, his face drawn, as if pulled suddenly back from a quiet contemplation. 'Justin, you might as well hear the rest of it,' Ford said, drawing him out to the veranda.

'I don't want to talk about it now,' Justin said wearily. 'Let's leave it lay for the present.'

Ford's face was angry. 'You might as well know that I didn't jump those three men—her former husband and those other two—because I was scared white. Go ahead, say it. Say I'm gutless.'

Justin stared at the tense face of his brother. 'Kid, there isn't a man alive who isn't gutless at one time or another.'

Slowly the tension left Ford's shoulders. 'You haven't called me "kid" since I was twelve years old.'

'That's right, I haven't.' Thoughtfully Justin stared at clouds thickening up in the east. 'It's eleven years ago this month. In February.'

'You'd have married her and had kids by now if—' Ford's voice broke. 'If it hadn't been for what I did.'

'It's the first time you ever told me that you were sorry for what happened, in so many words.'

Tears came to Ford's eyes, but his teeth were clenched in anger. 'Goddam it, Justin? I tried to tell you. I tried so many times I got

149

sick of trying. But you wouldn't listen. You never listen to anybody!'

'I have some riding to do, Ford.' Justin started for the bunkhouse to get his hat and gun and coat.

Ford fell in step with him. 'Justin, one more thing.'

Justin halted. 'Yes?'

'I tore up my copy of the agreement. I'm asking you to tear up yours.'

'You won this ranch fair and square. I lost the Ketcher place to the bank.'

'I'm not trying to be noble. But I can't run this place without your help.'

'There's not much to run now, kid.'

'I'm asking you to take your half.'

'I've got other things to think about first.' Across the yard, Ivy was emptying a pan of water. Justin watched her turn disconsolately back to the house. 'I shouldn't have brought her here,' Justin said under his breath. Hurt touched his eyes. 'I led her on, pretending I didn't know what she was. It was wrong.'

Ford tried to laugh. 'The way you talk, you'd think a Bible-shouter had been through here and baptized you in the horse trough.'

'Don't think I got holy all of a sudden.'

'I just never saw you this way before, Justin.'

'They call this the White Ruin, this blizzard,' Justin said. 'A lot of good men rode the pale horse in those hellish days. Things will never be quite the same again. Makes a man

150

sometimes take a minute to look deep inside himself.'

In the bunkhouse, Darsie Polk leaned on his homemade crutch. He watched in silence as Justin belted on a gun, put on his hat and leather coat, then picked up a rifle.

The foreman said, 'I figure I know where you're goin'.'

'I'm long overdue, Darsie. I won't be back until I finish it.'

'She ain't worth it.'

Justin halted in the doorway. 'Darsie, you asked me once to forgive Ford. Because you said every man had something on his conscience, something to live down.'

'But this is different.'

Justin shook his head. 'Ford had his burden and lived through it. And I hope I live through mine.' Justin looked the old man in the eye. 'The night you gave your watch to the Kiowa set me to thinking.'

For a moment Polk's face was set. Then his mouth relaxed. 'If this is what you want, I wish you luck.'

'It's what I want, Darsie.'

'Then I hope you bring her home with you.'

Justin rode in the direction of Midpoint.

Ivy, in the yard, watched him go. She stood with her small teeth sunk in her lip. Ford came to stand beside her, staring after Justin.

After a minute Ivy said, 'He's gone to try and find her.'

151

'You know this for sure?'

'It's a feeling I have.' Ivy took a deep breath. 'He still loves her.'

'And this you also know for sure?'

'He told me last night.'

CHAPTER TWENTY

Samantha read of the Great White Ruin in the pages of the *Silver City Blade*. From Wyoming to the Bend, tens of thousands of head of cattle lay dead upon the frozen ground. Hopsberg of the RB, worth a million in '85, now owed that much and more. Hundreds of the raggedy pants outfits were bankrupt. In the account she saw that Justin Emery had been wiped out. The Ketcher place was taken over by the Dearborn Livestock Bank of Chicago. It mentioned Ford Emery, owner of the Hayfork ranch at Midpoint, Texas, with dead cattle by the hundreds.

Everywhere there was chaos. Robertson of the Panhandle Cattlemen's Association declared that the cattle business was ruined. One of the greatest tragedies, the newspaper account stated, was the drift fence across the northern Panhandle, built at the instigation of the late Major Bert Emery of Hayfork. Cattle humping their tails, heads lowered, had drifted south in one great mass migration. Hundreds of them had been caught by the fence, where they froze to death. One rider reported dead cattle as far as a man could see.

Samantha, sitting at a window in the two-room shack at Las Rosas Mine, stared out at the miles of juniper-clad slopes of the Mogollons. Through the trees she could see the patches of snow that the New Mexican sun, on this winter day, could not reach. Below the shack and across an icy stream was the mine tunnel. A heavy plank door with bolted metal plates was ajar. It could close off the tunnel, but Erd had removed the hasp so there would be no danger of anyone's locking him inside the mine.

She could see him now, sitting on a rock near the footbridge. He was smoking a cigar. Kelso Kane was inspecting a chunk of ore Charlie Ivory had brought out of the tunnel.

With a heavy heart she pushed aside the newspaper she had been reading. Justin was bankrupt, but Ford was still reasonably solvent. And it was all her fault, the whole thing. Had it not been for her there would have been no fight between Ford and Justin, no reason to split the ranches. Her fault, not because she had married Justin, but because she had lied. A white lie, she had tried to tell herself at the time.

Mrs. Samantha Quine, widow.

Not Mrs. Samantha Quine, a woman who had disgraced the institution of marriage by divorcing her husband. No matter what the circumstances, the stigma remained.

Through the window she saw Erd sling the rifle under his arm, cross the footbridge, and start up the steep path to the shack. He threw his half-finished cigar over his shoulder, into the creek. He wore a wool shirt and a heavy jacket and high-laced boots. The successful mine owner! she thought. She had never learned how he had acquired Las Rosas Mine.

They'd come up through Mesilla, then Silver City. Three weeks ago they came to Mogollon, then deeper into the mountains to inspect the mine. Despite the winter, Erd wanted to see with his own eyes the value of his new possession. Probably it had been won in a card game in Mogollon; that was the logical explanation.

She remembered well the first time she learned he was a thief with cards. They had been married two weeks and were living at Paso Del Norte, where Erd was supposed to have an interest in a cattle company.

In the dead of night some men broke into her hotel room demanding to see Erd Quine. They carried rifles. She was terrified. As she sat up in bed, holding a blanket to her chin, the leader of the group said she was to tell Erd Quine that if he ever came back to Paso he would be shot on sight.

'What in the world did he do?' she managed to ask.

'He used his thief's slick fingers to double deal old man Holmby out of five hundred head of beef.'

Erd had not come to the hotel that night. For a week she had no word from him. Her money was gone and she was frantic. Then she received a letter from Tucson, and a hundred dollars. He told her to join him there.

When she finally confronted him with the accusation made by the men that night, he readily admitted it. 'I learned at an early age that I had a certain dexterity with my hands,' Erd said. 'A man fool enough to gamble with a stranger deserves to lose his money.'

'But he was an old man, they said.'

Erd smiled, never more charming, and drove her in a rented buggy to a house in a better part of town. 'I'll make it a point to gamble only with the younger men, if that'll make you happier.' He laughed.

They left Tucson in the middle of a rain-swept night, in a wagon with Erd whipping the team. Finally they slept under a tarp, with rain pattering on the canvas.

'Is this the way it's always going to be, Erd? Running like this?'

'You'll get used to it,' he had said indifferently.

'What did you do this time?'

But he was asleep and did not answer.

They took up residence in Prescott and for a time their lives were reasonably stable. Erd's

155

father had been one of the early settlers. Here people seemed more indulgent toward Erd, and he behaved himself. He worked for Senson and Harris, cattle buyers. He bought a new buggy and a team of high-stepping chestnuts.

It was at this time that Ron McCallum also went to work for the same company.

He was a tall, rather handsome man whose looks were spoiled only when he opened his mouth and displayed prominent gold teeth. His wife was a dumpy, plain little woman.

The moment McCallum laid eyes on Samantha he seemed intent on making her his personal project. He dogged her footsteps. Several times, when McCallum and his wife came for dinner, he kissed Samantha forcibly if he caught her alone in the kitchen. Once he tore her dress, even as, much later, Ford had done that day at Hayfork.

When McCallum was fired from Senson and Harris, Samantha hoped the unpleasantness would come to an end. His discharge was said to be for some double dealing in the buying or selling of cattle. Samantha was never sure just what it was, but it was obvious that McCallum was a thief. Even then, despite all she knew about Erd, she was reluctant to apply the same label to her own husband.

But McCallum did not leave town, as Samantha had hoped. One day his wife confronted Samantha in front of Dormeier's

Dry Goods. 'You are leading my husband on!' she had cried. 'You stop it, you hear?' She shook her fist. 'You stop it!'

A crowd had gathered, and Samantha found herself speechless with humiliation. She fled.

That night Erd, who seemed to be under some sort of pressure these days, told her almost the same thing. 'You're what we call a well-endowed woman,' he said, his teeth gleaming under the mustache. 'So why insist on wearing a tight dress every time McCallum is around?'

She was stunned. 'Erd, how can you say such a thing? I dress no differently when he's around.' She began to weep in frustration and rage.

'Next time you complain about the way I make my living, take a look in the mirror. Perhaps you'll see a face not quite as holy as you would like the world to believe.'

'Erd, listen to me.' They were in the parlor with the curtains drawn against the night. Only a single lamp was burning, on the cherrywood table. The glass shade was decorated with cherubs. 'I detest Ron McCallum. I put up with him only because he was your friend. Or so I thought. For your information, he's forced himself on me in this very house—'

'Forced himself? How interesting. To what degree did he force himself, may I ask?'

'He only kissed me. I would have said something to you, only—'

157

'Only you decided, why spoil things for yourself?'

'Erd, you know that isn't true.' His attitude shocked her. 'Why are you doing this to me?'

'An errant wife can sometimes drive a man to the verge of madness.'

'Erd!'

'Even the best personalities can crumple under such a strain!' He was shouting now.

Suddenly she realized what he meant. She sank back in the chair, speechless for a moment, her breath coming hard, as if he had struck her in the solar plexus with his fists. For several moments they sat staring across the table at each other. For the first time she really studied him in the wash of lamplight—the sullen eyes, the spoiled mouth under the mustache.

When she felt her voice would be reasonably steady, she cleared her throat. 'Erd, I'm not a fool.'

'No, that you aren't. You're a clever woman.'

'Oh, stop it!'

'You'd have to be for you and McCallum to carry on practically under my nose.'

'Did you spread your poison to his wife?' And when Erd just looked at her, she went on, 'Mrs. McCallum accused me today in public.'

'The injured wife. Why shouldn't she?'

'I sense what you're up to, Erd.'

His eyes widened a trifle, then narrowed.

158

'Now don't try and shift the blame to me.' He looked away.

'You're in some sort of trouble at Senson and Harris. McCallum was fired. I have a feeling you were in it together.'

'Nonsense!'

'Are you trying to build up these lies so that you can have an excuse to murder McCallum? Is that what you intend?' She rose, hands on the table, her entire body shaking. 'So perhaps he can't testify against you in court, or in some way reveal your hand in the mess?'

She stared down at his handsome face, waiting for him to strike her—or to deny it. But he sat quietly, rubbing his chin. Lamplight touched his sandy hair, his mustache. He was at that moment the ponderous thinker.

'Is the whole thing that transparent?' he asked, not to her, but to himself.

She was astounded. 'You admit it!'

For a moment he glared; then his mouth softened into the charming smile that had so attracted her at first. 'I was just testing a theory. To see if such a thing might be possible.'

He tried to catch her hands, but she jerked them out of his reach. 'You *do* admit it,' she repeated, breathing hard. 'Your own wife! You'd spread lies about your wife to cover up your own—'

'Samantha, you've gone quite far enough,' he stated coldly, rising from his chair. 'We'll

159

drop the subject, if you don't mind!'

As he left the house she screamed at him, 'I hate you. I hate you!'

That night, three hours later, shortly past eleven o'clock, Ron McCallum was shot in the back.

Erd was arrested at Hoberg's Livery Stable, where he was attempting to swap two matched chestnuts and a new buggy for a good saddle horse, a pack mule and a rifle.

At the trial, neighbors told of hearing loud quarreling at the Quine residence on the night of the murder. 'A man driven to the edge of madness by his wife,' said the attorney for the defense.

All eyes in the courtroom centered on Samantha.

She did not look at Erd even when the Territory demanded 'death by hanging.' But sympathy was obviously for Erd Quine, son of a pioneer, husband to a bitch wife. Then the verdict was brought in and Erd was taken away to Yuma Prison.

'If only he hadn't shot that rascal McCallum in the back. In the back—that's what made it bad for him.'

A further burden of shame had been placed upon Samantha's shoulders when she asked for a divorce. Because of the stories about her, she could not walk down the street without some reference being made concerning 'loose women.' When the divorce was granted, she left Prescott, giving no forwarding address. She went to St. Louis and became the Widow Quine, widowhood not being such a social blight as divorce.

Only later did it turn out that a rancher named Childers, dying of lung fever, had killed McCallum because McCallum had cheated him out of his life savings in a cattle swindle.

Now Erd entered the shack, brushing some of the New Mexican snow from his hat. His face was tanned and healthy. Prison had tightened his mouth, put creases at the corners of his eyes. But he was still as debonair as ever.

He glanced at the newspaper she had been reading; Charlie Ivory had brought it from Mogollon last night.

'I see you've had the news,' Erd Quine said, leaning his rifle against the wall. 'So Emery didn't die after all.'

'I knew he wouldn't die.'

'Well, I lost interest in him when the cattle business went to pieces. He's broke like the rest of them.'

Samantha said nothing.

'You got out just in time,' Quine went on. 'Wife to a bankrupt rancher.'

She stared at his new boots. She'd heard Erd and the other two discussing the mine property. Already nearly seven thousand dollars had been taken out.

'Justin may be bankrupt,' she said, 'but at least he's not a thief.'

161

He tapped his forehead. 'Takes brains to be a good thief. Emery wouldn't even know where to start.' He grinned.

'That night at Paso, when those men broke into my room and accused you of being a cheat, I refused to believe them. I see you haven't changed any.'

'Don't irritate me too much. I might do something drastic. Such as letting Kelso be the one to discipline you.'

She turned white and looked away. Whenever she was alone at the camp with Kelso Kane she was frightened. At least Charlie Ivory treated her with a shred of respect. Kane just stared at her in that sullen way that was more effective than if he actually voiced what she knew to be on his mind.

'Why in the world did I ever come here with you?' she cried.

'Because you bargained for Justin Emery's life, and I listened to you.'

'Listened to me only because you finally got it through your head that I'd be his widow if he died, and it would be better if he died of natural causes.'

'I should have killed him.' Erd's lips twisted. 'The farther south we came and heard the talk and saw the dead cattle, I knew he was broke. I didn't have to read a newspaper to learn that.'

She took a deep breath. 'Erd, I think you'd better take me to Silver City.'

'And why should I do that?'

'We despise each other.'

'So we do.'

'There is no reason for us to continue this stupidity of pretending we're still man and wife.'

'The stupidity, as you call it,' he said, giving her a thin smile, 'has its pleasures.'

'Nothing you can say will embarrass me. By marrying you in the first place I accepted the brand of a wanton.'

'The wanton was born in you. I had nothing to do with that.'

She shook her head. 'You're wrong. The night those men broke into my room—would they have done that to a woman they considered decent? No. Because I was Mrs. Erdman Quine, they—'

'Remember what Shakespeare said? Something about protesting too much?'

'Erd, I intend leaving here.'

'Fine. I'll tell Kelso to escort you to town. I believe he would cut off a thumb if I told him that was what it would take to get you.'

She folded the newspaper and took it across the room to a desk. She didn't want to give Erd the satisfaction of seeing the fear in her eyes. Kelso Kane had never so much as touched her arm with the tip of a finger; it was his manner that terrified her. She felt goosepimples break out on her forearms.

It was Erd's idea of a joke, to keep her constantly under pressure, with the four of them spending so much time together under one roof. Kane and Ivory bunked here in the parlor, the Quines had the small room that passed for a bedroom. But all were under the one roof.

'Erd, just how long do you think you can go on like this without something giving way?'

'You mean three men and one woman?' The idea seemed to amuse him.

'Why are you this way, Erd? What did I ever do to you?'

His face tightened. 'You ruined my life.'

'I wasn't the one who stole, who cheated others. It was you who did those things.'

'I spent three years in Yuma Prison.'

'How can you blame that on me?' she cried.

'For this simple reason,' he said, through his teeth. 'Because I refuse to blame anything on myself. Anything at all.'

She shook her pale head in bewilderment. 'One thing about you that always amazed me was your frankness.'

'You'd better start supper.'

'Erd, won't you help me get out of these mountains? Won't you do that one decent thing for me?'

'So you can run back to Justin Emery?' he snapped.

'I will never go back to him,' she said, wiping her eyes with the tips of her fingers.

'You still love him.'

She felt utterly whipped. 'Without me he

164

has a chance to save himself. He can devote himself to salvaging what he can, and not have the burden of me.' She swallowed and felt a stinging pressure of tears again behind her eyelids.

'Tell me,' Erd said after a moment, 'just how many times did you and Ford Emery—' He broke off, laughing, as he heard footsteps.

Kelso Kane had come up the path and now he paused just inside the door. Behind him loomed Charlie Ivory.

Erd said an insane thing. 'It would be something if we all got snowbound here for a week or more and couldn't get out of the house.'

Kelso Kane's eyes in the brown face flicked from Samantha to Erd, then back again. He said nothing. He only looked at her steadily until she was sure the hammer beat of her heart carried clear across the room.

Charlie Ivory, crowding into the shack, said, 'If we'd stayed at Princess Station we'd have been snowbound sure as hell.'

'We should've stayed there,' Kelso Kane said, and looked at Samantha's breasts.

Later, when the dishes were done, she had to get outside. She put on a heavy coat against the bitter mountain night. Upon leaving the shack, she tried to determine which of the many trails branching off into the wilderness would lead to civilization.

Erd Quine followed her, closing the door

behind him. 'Planning to walk to Mogollon? Or maybe clear to Silver City?'

She turned, hands clenched in the thickness of the coat. 'Erd, if you want to toy with me, keep me on edge, that's one thing. But it's madness to keep goading Kelso that way.'

'Like I told you once, I didn't have much to think about at Yuma. But now I'm enjoying myself. It's like a play, with me the audience. Watching the three of you—'

'I suppose your greatest satisfaction will be the day they finally take me.'

He shook his head. 'It'll never come to that.' His voice hardened. 'I'd kill them both, and they know it.'

'Then why in the world—'

'Why keep it up? Maybe to see how much pressure the three of you can stand.'

'You're mad.'

'Not at all. It's the same sort of pressure you get in prison. The kind nobody talks about. We had a guard named Simmons. He would stand outside the cell door and tell about the girls he had, and what they did, and then he'd laugh at us. Maybe that doesn't sound like much to you.'

'Erd, I know you suffered in prison, but won't you let me go my own way? You care nothing for me.'

'And you care nothing for me, of course.'

'Erd, I did love you once. You killed it.'

'Your love doesn't particularly interest me,

Samantha. You're a prize that other men want. Maybe one day, when they cease to want you, I'll let you go.'

Somehow she had to get away from him. Just how this could be managed, she didn't know at the moment. But a way would present itself. Her best plan would be to get into Mexico. She had lived there as a girl; she knew the country, she could speak the language.

And she had heard gossip, when they were in Mesilla, that some of those previously discredited by Diaz were now back in his favor. The LePages had had many friends in Chihuahua City. In some way they would make a place for her.

Erd seemed to read her thoughts. 'Don't try to get away. Kelso could track a tarantula across solid rock. I'll send him after you.'

She stepped into the shack, her heart pounding.

CHAPTER TWENTY-ONE

Justin stopped off in Midpoint. In the office of Edgar Dobbs, the lawyer said, 'Ford has told you he can't bring back Hayfork by himself. He needs you.'

'He's more generous than I would be under the circumstances,' Justin said. He stared out the window, down at Houston, the main street of Midpoint. The two new buildings of cut stone remained half finished, the walls irregular the way the masons had left them when the golden spring of cattle money suddenly went dry. Some said the buildings would never be completed now.

Cowmen gathered in tense little groups along the walks, trying to glean any rumor of hope from those who had come in from swings around the country, visiting other spreads.

Dobbs hitched himself forward in his chair. 'Give Ford this chance to prove himself to you.'

'He saved my life. That puts me forever in his debt.'

'That isn't the same,' Dobbs said with a shake of his head. 'That's only what any decent person would do—try to save the life of another human being, if at all possible. No, this other would give Ford the satisfaction of knowing that you had forgiven him at last.'

'It's so far in the past, what difference does it make now?'

'But far in the past or not,' Dobbs went on, grinding his back teeth on a knob of tobacco, 'you never did forgive him.'

'No, I guess I didn't. Not really.'

'Then do this one thing. Let him make this gesture. It won't bring Elsie back to life, but it will make Ford realize you have forgiven him for it.'

'If we did team up again, what is there left

to salvage?'

'The Major fought back from as bad circumstances. Many times.' Dobbs hooked a cuspidor with his instep and hauled it within range, then let go. Wiping his lips, he said, 'The Major lost most of his cows to them Missouri bastards, driving to Joplin one year. He was hit by drought and bad times. The year your mother died he was drunk for most of the next twelve months.'

'I'd forgotten that.'

'Around here they said he was through; at least some of them did. They were ready to grab Hayfork, but he sobered up and fought back.'

'Funny, I never remember calling my father anything but the Major. I guess I didn't miss sentiment so much, because I was always working. But Ford—maybe he did miss it. Maybe that's why he had to show off. Like he did that day with Elsie.'

'You have to remember that things were different in those days, Justin. A widower with two boys to raise didn't have much time for sentiment. A man spent all his energy on just staying alive.'

Justin stood up and again looked down into the street, seeing the drawn faces of the men, the fear-ridden way the women held to the hands of their young children.

'I hear Cob Shandy shot himself,' Justin said.

'That's one way to solve the problem, Justin.'

'I was damn sorry to hear about Cob.'

'He just couldn't bring himself to accept the fact that it was only in the last ten years he rode high in the saddle. He forgot that when he came out of the war all he had was an old gun, a few Jeff Davis dollars, and a mule. He couldn't go back and do it all over.' Dobbs sighed. 'A lot of us are going to have to do that, Justin.'

'You were smart to buy a diamond ring, Edgar.'

Dobbs rubbed the finger that still bore a slight indentation from the metal band. 'We're eating off it, Justin. We're luckier than most.'

'I suppose.'

'The Ketcher place is gone and there's nothing you can do about that. The banks had to pull in what they could in a hurry, or they'd go bust like the cowmen.'

'They pulled in awful fast.'

'You still have the Midpoint place. You can hold a roundup. Might be you'll have more cows than you figure.'

'That's something Ford and Darsie can do. I've got a job to do first. Go fetch my wife.' He stepped to the door. 'Thanks for finding that letter for me, Edgar.'

'Postmark of Mesilla won't mean too much. Could have been mailed when she was passing through.'

170

'She's the kind of a woman someone will remember seeing,' Justin said. 'Once you see her, you'd never forget her.'

'Good luck, Justin. If it's what you want, I hope you locate her.'

'Just keep it under your hat. I'll appreciate it.'

'You're my client and I'm a lawyer. I don't talk about what goes on between us.'

'I know that.'

Justin crossed over to Teakant's and had a drink and listened to the doleful discussions of the Great White Ruin.

'You hear about Cob Shandy?' Teakant asked.

'Damn shame. I liked Cob a lot.'

'Is Mrs. Emery enjoying her stay in St. Louis?'

Justin said, 'She'll be home one of these days.'

'Say, I hate to bring this up, Justin, and I reckon Ford's forgot about it.' Teakant chewed a cold cigar for a moment as if trying to frame appropriate words for a distasteful subject. 'Ford took a rifle and a revolver from me and promised to pay. It was while you was uptrail, heading for the Ketcher place. It was after them three fellas was here and Ford went to warn you. At least, that's where we figured he went.'

'That's where he went,' Justin said.

'I wouldn't say anything, but—' Teakant

gave him a sad smile. 'But times are hard. I'm carrying half the boys in Midpoint now. I wouldn't bother you, but Ford doesn't come in no more and I never had a chance to bring it up to him.'

'Ford hasn't been in for a drink?'

'Not since he come back.'

'You'll get your money, Lew.' Justin pushed himself back from the bar. 'I have to make a business trip to Mesilla. I need what cash I have at the moment. We'll settle up when I get back. Ford and I are partners again.'

'Damn glad to hear that, Justin. Ford's lookin' right well. Saw him in town the other day, but didn't want to bust out of here and ask about money when he was with the young lady.'

'Young lady?'

'You know, her being a lady and all. And maybe her not knowing that Ford ever came to a place like this.' When Justin stared at him blankly for a moment, Teakant went on, 'The young lady Ford brought to town. Edgar says she's shirttail kin of yours.'

'Oh, you mean Ivy. Yes, she's what you might call shirttail kin.'

'Maybe that's why Ford's quit drinkin'.' Teakant smiled. 'Influence of a good woman on a man has brought more'n one saloon to ruin.'

'I suppose.'

'The young lady resembles Elsie Gorman—

172

begging your pardon, Justin, for bringing that up. But some of us were talking about it the other day, how much this girl reminds us of Elsie.'

'Lew, I'll see you when I get back from Mesilla.'

But Teakant was shaking his head, looking mournful, adding, 'Doesn't seem right, Elsie being gone. Why you and her would've been married for years and had a passel of younguns by now. Elsie and the other ladies of the town would—'

Something hot and ugly rolled up into Justin's throat. 'Lew, shut your goddam mouth!'

Others in the Rainbow heard him and turned to stare in surprise.

Teakant's mouth fell open and his cigar dropped onto the bar. It lay there like a stub of soggy rope. 'My God, Justin, I never meant nothing!'

Justin took a backward step, the rest of his restraint breaking in him like thin glass. *The influence of a good woman!*'

'Justin, I shouldn't have brung up Elsie.'

Justin whirled on the others, his face livid. 'You never liked my wife, not one of you. But Samantha Emery is the best woman who ever breathed Midpoint air.'

He stormed out, swinging shut the winter doors with such force the narrow glass inserts rattled in their frames.

'I never in my life heard Justin bellow like that,' said one man, awed by what he had seen.

'It must be the Major comin' alive in him after all this time,' another said. 'Justin always held himself in till now.'

'What did I say?' Teakant looked bewildered. 'I only said that girl of Ford's reminded me of Elsie Gorman. I said maybe it was the influence of a good woman that made Ford stop drinking. I never said anything against his wife.'

'Let's face a fact, gentlemen,' said Solly Granger of the Midpoint Stable, coming to the bar from a corner where he had been playing solitaire. 'There isn't a man in this room that hasn't at one time or another considered Samantha Emery a hussy.'

This was greeted by an indignant silence for a moment, and then the men exchanged glances. The silence grew strained and they shuffled their feet awkwardly and cleared their throats.

Edgar Dobbs, who had seen Justin spur his horse out of town at a dead run, had come over to see what caused the sudden exit from Teakant's Rainbow.

When the matter was explained, Dobbs said, 'Solly's right. I reckon we've all had our private opinions of Mrs. Emery. Much as we tried to hold in for Justin's sake, some of it was bound to show through.'

'But why did he blow up, after all this time?'

asked a man at the bar.

'Reckon it was on account of a letter I showed him,' Dobbs said.

'What letter?'

'Samantha knew the ladies of the town didn't like her. That includes my wife. But in spite of that, Samantha wanted to do a favor for—' Dobbs broke off. 'I already said too much.'

They tried to get the rest of it out of Dobbs, but he refused to discuss the matter further.

'I hate all this, for Justin's sake,' Solly Granger muttered, and turned his hot gaze on Teakant. 'Lew, why in hell did you have to bring up the fact that we thought Ford's girl reminds us of Elsie Gorman? No matter what Edgar says, I think that's what started the thing.'

Teakant shrugged. 'A saloonman gets in the habit of talking to customers and not paying much attention to what he says.'

'From now on you better listen to yourself talk,' Granger advised. 'Or one day a customer will put a bullet in your head and you'll never know why he shot you.'

'I suggest,' said Edgar Dobbs, pushing his round little figure up to the bar, 'that when Mrs. Emery returns from St. Louis, we go out of our way to make her feel welcome.'

'It's the womenfolks you'll have to convince,' a man said.

'If we'd all quit talking about Mrs. Emery,'

175

Edgar Dobbs said, 'and twisting our heads around till our necks like to crack every time Mrs. Emery walks down the street, maybe the other ladies would quit resenting her so.'

'Reckon there's such a thing as a woman bein' too easy on the eyes?' Teakant asked.

'God sure put it all in Mrs. Emery, that's for certain,' said another.

'The good Lord might make a mistake here and there,' Solly Granger said, 'but He sure was watching His business when He fashioned up Samantha Emery.'

'I say let's drink to the lady's health,' Edgar Dobbs said, looking around. 'And I do mean lady.'

'And while we're at it,' said Solly Granger, 'let's drink to Miss Ivy in memory of Elsie Gorman.'

A girl's voice came plaintively from the foot of the stairway, beyond the portiere at the end of the bar: 'Is Ford Emery going to marry that girl?'

'Helen, get back upstairs,' Teakant said sourly. 'You know better'n to show your face down here.'

'I just asked about Ford. Is there any harm in that? He never comes in these days and I—'

'Her and Ford used to sit up there, and Ford would get drunk and talk the night through,' Teakant explained to the others.

'One thing for sure, Helen,' a man said, 'Ford ain't about to climb your back stairs

176

while he's got Miss Ivy on his arm.'

'Go on back upstairs now, Helen,' Lew Teakant said, his voice milder, but insistent. 'You know the rules.'

A man asked, 'What'd you and Ford talk about all night, anyhow?'

'That Elsie Gorman. Ford would tell about the horses and how they ran away and how Elsie fell out of the wagon. And how Justin beat him that day. And later the Major took a buggy whip and whipped the shirt off his back.'

'I never knew the Major whupped him for it,' said Granger. 'Ford was only a show-off boy. He didn't mean to see her dead.'

'I used to tell Ford that,' said Helen through the portiere. 'But he would say he got what he deserved. He was always trying to make it up to his brother and the Major, but everything just went wrong for him, every time he tried.'

'Tried too hard, likely,' Dobbs said.

'Biggest funeral this town ever had,' mused Lew Teakant. 'And the coffin nailed shut, her bein' in such poor shape.'

'Wish you was marrying Ford, huh, Helen?' said a man, easing the somber atmosphere with a laugh.

'Now you're making fun of me. I only meant if he is marrying her, I hope he's happy. I saw them together from the window. She's pretty.'

A cowpuncher hitched up his pants and swaggered toward the end of the bar. 'Get on up there, Helen, and I'll be right behind you. I sure as hell ain't goin' to talk all night. I got other things planned.'

The men laughed and for a moment the tension eased. They were able to forget that for the first time since the War Between the States a Texas cowman was about the poorest mortal walking God's earth in a pair of boots.

CHAPTER TWENTY-TWO

Everywhere Justin rode he heard dire predictions concerning the cattle business. At the Drover's Bar off the plaza in Mesilla, a man said, 'Nobody but a fool would raise cows after this blasted winter. The public will have to learn to live without beef and eat grass.'

Justin was on his second drink at the crowded bar. 'Does the name Quine mean anything to any of you boys?'

The men turned to stare at him through a fog of tobacco smoke. Some of them exchanged glances.

'Can't say I ever heard the name, mister. You a Pinkerton man or something?'

'The name is Emery.'

'Well, why in the hell didn't you say so? A Texas Emery, I'm assuming.'

'Hayfork. Midpoint, Texas.'

'Knowed the Major. Fine man.'

'It was the Major prodded the boys to build

that goddam Panhandle drift fence,' shouted a red-faced little man, who was obviously drunk. 'I lost eight hundred head when they drifted south and froze solid on that cussed bob wire.'

The bartender said, 'Shut up, Eddie.'

'I wouldn't give you any information, Emery,' Eddie spluttered, 'if you paid me in Chicago gold.'

'What information?' Justin said, aware of a quickening interest.

'Hah! You'd like to get it out of me. The hell with you!'

The men formed an aisle between the two. They watched, sensing excitement.

Justin was thoughtful for a moment. 'The only information I need is the whereabouts of a man named Erdman Quine.'

'That's the information I mean.' Eddie grinned.

'Tell me—'

'Hah!' The little man slapped his hand on the edge of a deal table in his exuberance. 'Wouldn't tell an Emery one goddam thing. On account of your father.' He shook a fist at Justin, his face twisting in anger. 'He cost me eight hundred head.'

'Quine had nothing to do with that fence,' Justin parried, his voice carrying in the stillness: 'How could he? He's a druggist from Abilene.'

'He's a tinhorn!'

'You're insulting a friend!'

179

'Good. If he's a friend of yours, I'll insult him further. He stole a mine from a poor Mex bastard up at Romero's. Silver City, I think it was.'

'Thanks very much,' said Justin. He put a coin on the bar. 'Buy Eddie a drink, with my compliments.'

CHAPTER TWENTY-THREE

One morning at breakfast Erd Quine said, 'I believe I can get a good price for the mine, come spring.'

Charlie Ivory held a cup of coffee in his oversized hand. 'Why not work it ourselves?'

Quine gave the big man an indulgent smile. 'You and Kelso can break your backs on it. But I find there are easier ways to make a living.'

Kelso Kane was hunched at the table, his dark face inscrutable. He was staring at Samantha as she turned a fresh batch of flapjacks at the stove.

Although Samantha stood with her back to the table, she could feel Kane's eyes on her. It put a small flutter of fear in her throat. But when she placed the flapjacks on the table and sat down next to Erd, she managed to make her face impassive.

Across the room, so near and yet a thousand miles away, was Erd's rifle. What could she do if she did manage to get her hands on it? Kill them? No, she was not quite up to that, unless it was in defense of her person. And if it did come to this, she wondered if she would be conscience stricken at all. There would be no reason to be. She had suffered enough humiliation and mental torture at their hands.

If she did get the rifle she could perhaps hold them at bay until she got a horse. But she didn't know the mountain trails. They could easily run her down, and then what? They could come in on her from three sides.

And if Erd somehow was the one killed and she was left alone with the other two—She shivered. Was there really much choice?

Charlie Ivory looked out the window. 'It's startin' to snow. Maybe another blizzard.'

Kelso Kane gave a snort of laughter.

'Kelso, what's so funny?' Quine demanded.

'You said yourself the other day, what if we was all snowed in here?' His bright eyes lifted to Samantha's across the table.

'It's all right for me to talk about it,' Quine said, his mouth tight under the mustache. 'The same doesn't go for you!'

Kane stared at him through a film of steam rising from the stack of flapjacks. After a moment Kane lowered his gaze. Quine seemed pleased that he had outstared him.

But the snow turned out to be no blizzard. By ten o'clock it had stopped and a wan sun shone down through the junipers and flashed on the icy creek under the footbridge. Samantha longed for spring. Never had she longed for anything more, except to push back time to that November day when she had received the brief note from Mary Hope: '. . . a man claiming to be your husband . . .'

It was her fault, hers alone, for not forcing Justin to accept the fact that she had lied to him. Lied about Erdman Quine, not dead, but alive. Samantha not a widow, but a woman divorced. There had been the fear that Justin, so preoccupied with the cattle business, might despise her when he realized what she had done, but even that would have been preferable to what followed. Justin would not have broken with Ford and trailed a herd north, where it was caught by the great blizzard.

Erd Quine stayed behind when Ivory and Kane went down to the mine. 'Something just occurred to me,' he said. 'You have connections in Mexico.'

'What connections?' she said, wondering what devilment he proposed this time.

'You lived there with the LePages. They were big people in Chihuahua City.'

'Erd, what are you leading up to?'

'You know people down there. And you can get word to some of them that we have Yankee cattle to sell. The price is very cheap.'

'How can you do that?' she asked, trying to give herself time to think.

'When cows cost you nothing you can sell under the market price.' He smiled. 'Way under.'

Suddenly she caught a glimmer of what he had in mind. 'No, I'm not going to do it.'

'Of course you're going to do it. You get word to Justin Emery to meet you at Quintero. It's south and east of Paso Del Norte.'

'I'm quite aware of the location,' she said thinly.

'Tell Emery to meet you there with a thousand head of Hayfork cows. If he doesn't have a thousand left, he can borrow, or he can rustle what he needs on the way down. Every Texan has swung a wide loop at one time or other in his life. It won't be anything new.'

'You're completely insane to think that—'

'And you'll use your influence to see that we have a buyer waiting for us in Mexico.'

'Justin no longer owns Hayfork.'

Erd laughed. 'He'll step on the neck of that gutless brother of his and take what he wants. I know his kind.'

Samantha looked into Erd Quine's hazel eyes. 'I suppose if I refuse, you'll contrive in some way to kill Justin.'

'This you know.'

'Erd, this isn't the sixties or the seventies. This is the eighties. Almost the last of this century. These things you plan can't be done today.'

'They're being done all the time.' He

laughed. 'This mine, for instance. A drunken Mexican plays a bad hand of poker and loses his mine.'

'Still the thief.'

He only smiled. 'I admit you couldn't do these things back east. Even in your precious St. Louis, perhaps. But this is still wild country. No matter how much you like to pretend that it's civilized, it won't be for another forty years.'

Samantha's tongue licked at her pale lips. 'Your plan has a flaw.'

'And just what is that?'

'Justin has no use for me. You'd be wasting your time trying to get him to deliver a herd on my say so.'

'Anything is a gamble. You get paper and write what I tell you.'

She hesitated, trying to think of a way to thwart him. In Mesilla she had managed to scribble a note to Maude Dobbs that might, if circulated sufficiently, help Ford to gain some degree of stature in the eyes of his neighbors. She felt it was the least she could do to make amends. It had been sheer torture not to ask that word be passed on to Justin that her love for him was undying, despite the tragedy of their lives. Or she could have written to Justin direct. However, this she could not bring herself to do.

And now Erd was demanding that she write him. If she did, Justin's opinion of her would be lowered even more. Couldn't Erd see that? A promiscuous wife fallen even deeper into the pit by being a party to blackmail—

Erd Quine sensed her hesitation. 'If at any point in your life you decide to completely defy me, I give you this solemn oath—I will devote my remaining years to one objective, the destruction of Justin Emery.'

She got a sheet of paper, a pen, and an inkwell, and waited at the table for him to dictate.

When she wrote 'Dear Justin,' she felt a dull pain in her breast. She wrote only a few of the dictated lines, then suddenly threw down the pen. 'Erd, I won't go on with it.' She fled into the bedroom, flung herself across the bed, and wept.

'Such spirit,' Erd said thinly from the doorway, 'must be rewarded.'

Strangely enough, he didn't press the matter.

Two mornings later, when she was alone in the shack, she happened to glance down at the mine entrance. The heavy plank door that usually stood ajar was now closed. It was held in place by a stout timber. One end of the timber was jammed under a rusted strip of iron on the door, the other end against a post in the ground that supported the far end of the footbridge.

Through her mind spun a question: Why was the mine door locked in this manner?

Then her heart froze. She was at the east window, with her back to the door. She heard the door open quietly, then close. Temptation to look around was almost overpowering, yet she steeled herself to show no outward fear.

She had no weapon, no way to defend herself. Only a butcher knife across the room. And she knew if she tried to reach it he'd block her.

She could scream and try to run, but it would be useless. Perhaps she could try and be clever. But she didn't feel clever. She was terrified.

Kelso Kane's voice reached her. 'I've waited a damn long time for this.'

'So have I,' she said, her voice reasonably steady. Desperately she fought for self-control, so that when she did face him there would be high color in her face, instead of paleness. Often she had been accused of playing the role, but in reality she found it most difficult.

'What'd you mean by that?' Kane demanded in a surly voice. 'You haven't been waiting at all for me.'

She turned. He stood across the room, his shoulders hunched, the lashings of the blanket coat dangling. The long brown face with the narrowed eyes was expressionless. She knew his gun was in the cut-down holster under the tail of the coat. But she did not lower her eyes to it. That would give her away.

The smile she forced felt ghastly upon her

186

lips. 'Yes, I've waited a long time. I began to think you weren't much of a man, not to take what you wanted. What I wanted.'

'You don't fool me none. I've seen the way you looked at me.'

'Under Erd's nose, why not?' She lifted a hand to smooth her yellow hair and saw that his eyes followed the movement with interest. 'You've seen him slap me. He'd do worse if he had any idea that I—' She let her voice fade tantalizingly. The tip of a pink tongue licked her lower lip.

'You're much woman,' he said.

'Much woman, yes. It's a thing the Spanish would say. Why don't you take me to Mexico?'

'Like I said, you don't fool me one damn bit.'

'Are they securely locked in the mine—Erd and Charlie?'

'If they weren't, I wouldn't waste time letting you try and talk me out of this. I'd get right at it.'

'Why do you think I'm trying to talk you out of it, Kelso?' she said, making her voice soft.

'You're tryin' not to look scared. But it shows.'

She gave a small laugh, tilting back her head, her wide blue eyes sweeping to him provocatively. 'You could at least carry me into the room. Or do you intend to make me walk?' She held out her hands to him.

He stood still. 'You figure to get your hand

on my gun.'

For a fleeting moment the terror squeezed off her breath. But her smile remained intact. No matter how she tried to outmaneuver him, he was there to counter. Desperation began to stir a wildness in her heart.

'You behave and you won't get hurt,' he said. 'You make me mad and there won't be a man alive will want to look at your face.'

She stared at him, the smile washed clear of her lips now.

'You believe me?' he insisted.

'I believe you,' she said hoarsely.

Swiftly he crossed the room and drew the butcher knife from its wooden slot near the stove. He threw the knife into the yard and closed the door.

'You've damn near drove me out of my mind these last weeks,' he told her.

'It wasn't my intention.' She took a backward step.

'I don't care if Erd hunts me down and tries to kill me. I figure to have what you been pushin' at me every time you crook a finger or touch your hair or just breathe.' His gaze lowered to her breasts. 'Yeah, even watchin' you take a long breath.'

Pivoting, she dashed for the bedroom. She slammed the door in his face and braced her body against the pressure of his shoulder. Gradually he forced the door, pushing her back. When it was nearly open she suddenly removed her own weight and spun for a window. Release of the door sent him sprawling into the room. She had the window half open when he caught her. He threw her across the bed and slammed down the window.

Then, in that moment of terror, when she lay frozen on the bed, Erd Quine's voice reached her. 'All right, Kelso. That's far enough.'

The words were not spoken in anger, but drawled. There in the doorway stood Erd. Behind him towered Charlie Ivory, trying to peer into the room. Kelso Kane had lost his hat when he fell into the room. Now he swept back his long black hair and picked up the hat.

For a moment he stared at the rifle in Erd Quine's hands. Then he looked around at Samantha, unsmiling. But he said to Erd, 'You were right. She was some scared; believe me she was.'

Quine gave a small laugh and stepped aside so Kane could leave the room.

'How could you do it, Erd?' she cried, her voice shaking as she got up from the bed. 'How could one human be so cruel—'

'Did you really think I was fool enough to let myself get locked up in that mine?' he drawled.

'Why do you do these things to me?'

'You don't know?'

'Is what I've done so terrible?'

'You didn't wait for me.'

189

'I was to wait the rest of my life for you?'

'Yes,' he stated, no longer laughing. 'You were my wife.' His mouth took on an ugly slant under his mustache. 'Kelso, you and Charlie clear out. One of you go fetch some supplies. The other one keep an eye out. I'm going to be busy for a spell.'

Ivory said, 'It's Sunday. No use goin' to town.'

'Show them money,' Erd snapped. 'They'll open the store.'

Ivory frowned. 'Romero ain't friendly. I don't know about goin'.'

'Romero will sweat and stew, and by the time be gets around to doing anything about the mine I'll have it sold.'

Ivory and Kane left the shack and went outside. In a moment there was the sound of a horse moving away from the mine, heading south.

'So this was your revenge,' she said numbly. 'Because I refused to write the letter to Justin.'

Erd Quine closed the door. 'Undress.'

'Erd, please—after what I've been through?'

'The clothes,' he said in a thin and dangerous voice. 'They come off whole or in rags. That's up to you.'

'Erd, please—'

'I swear to you—'

'All right. All *right*!'

She lay, wanting to weep. But she was now past tears.

190

He glared down at her. 'I shouldn't even touch you. You gave yourself to another man. Justin Emery!'

'I married him,' she said in a dull voice. 'He was my husband.'

Leaning over, he slapped her hard across the face so that her head was slammed deep into the straw mattress. 'Not your husband,' he said. 'You have only one husband in this lifetime. Me. Erdman Bixley Quine. The other man was your lover. Always remember that!'

She lay with her eyes closed, her cheek smarting where he had struck her.

'I want you to know this,' he went on, still using that venomous voice she had grown to fear. 'Even had I not been legally freed from Yuma, I would have escaped. Some day I would have found you. Remember that. When you married me, it was for all the days of your life.'

'What pleasure can this possibly give you?'

'Also remember this,' he said, ignoring her. 'Because of your stupid attitude in scorning me, I intend to shoot down Justin Emery. I'll wait till he's riding high again—you're so damn sure that he will. When that happens, when he's got his mountain of gold, I'll put him under the ground.'

'Yes, I suppose you will.'

'I'll do it the ugly way, Samantha. You know if I put my mind to it I can devise something—'

'Erd, do you know if I had to make a choice

at this moment between you or Kelso Kane—'

'Don't say it, Samantha,' he said quietly, 'because I'll give you to him. Then will come Charlie Ivory. I'll drag you from one corner of this territory to another. I'll find all the camps and the mines and the places where men don't see a woman from one year to the next.'

'You may plan this, and I know you will. But you remember something, Erd. I'd kill myself before I'd ever let you do that to me.'

'The purity of womanhood,' he laughed.

'Not for that reason at all. It's because I'm sick of your rottenness.'

'Why do you continue to defy me? You know you'll only be hurt for it.'

'So what is hurt? With death, even that passes.' She looked him in the eye. His death and hers, if necessary. It was the only way Justin would ever have a life for himself.

CHAPTER TWENTY-FOUR

Snow was packed in the deep ruts that had been chewed into the frozen ground by ore wagons. Ahead, through a screening of junipers, Justin could see the village of Mogollon. Smoke belching from numerous stacks laced the clear blue sky. The town itself was built on an incline. One end of the loading platform in front of Sewell and Smith's Store was on level ground, the other end twelve feet in the air; the grade was that steep. Some men lounging in front of the stamp mill in their Sunday coats turned to stare at him curiously. A lone rider in these mountains might mean any number of things. It was the sort of trail a man might take to flee the law.

Justin rode on up the street until he saw a sign: Romero's. He smiled to himself. In Silver City there were several people named Romero, but no place by that name. And no one had heard of a man named Quine, or a Mexican losing a mine to a tinhorn. Justin had felt defeated until a man said, 'There's a Romero's at Mogollon.'

Even then he wasn't sure until he had pushed into the high mountains. And here it was, before his eyes.

He swung down. Three other horses were at the rail, their breaths steaming, frost in their winter coats. Unfastening his coat, he hiked his revolver to an easier position, then entered the bar. A blast of heat from a sheet-iron stove struck his face.

Behind the bar, a fat Mexican with a cigarillo tucked back of his ear set out a bottle and a dirty glass. A dozen men ranged along the bar, wearing the high-laced boots of mining men. On a platform a bald man sat drinking from a stein of beer while picking out hymns with one finger on a piano keyboard.

Justin laid a coin on the bar. 'Are you

193

Romero?' he asked the Mexican.

The man stiffened. He was thick through the chest, his skull round, his nose flat. His small dark eyes studied Justin suspiciously. 'The sign out front mentions Romero,' he said. 'Who knows who he is?'

Justin said, 'I'm not a lawman, if that's what worries you.'

The big Mexican showed his teeth in a tight smile. 'A man says he is not the law, so that makes it so, eh?'

'I mean no trouble. I'm Justin Emery of Hayfork in Texas.'

'I've heard of Emery. You're bust now, eh? All cowmen bust.' The idea seemed to please him.

Some of the men down the bar had turned to stare. A stocky man with a fiery red beard gave Justin a sour look. 'Maybe now you Texans will see that it's the ore dug from the ground, not beef on the hoof, that makes the country prosper.'

Justin turned. 'People can't eat ore. They can eat beef.'

Justin's attempt at lightness did not reach the red-bearded man. 'You cowmen hold hands with the railroads,' he said thinly, 'and they do your bidding.'

'Depends on which side of the creek you're on,' Justin said. 'Just as many cowmen figure the miners and the railroads sleep in the same tent.'

194

'I've waited a long time for this,' the red-bearded man went on vehemently. 'To see the cattle interests bankrupt. They've been too high-handed.'

'In what way, may I ask?'

'Here in these mountains are certain cowmen who think they own the very water and ground staked out by a mining man.'

Justin poured himself a drink. 'I'm not here to argue the merits of your case.' He had his drink, shuddered, and turned to the big Mexican. 'I'm looking for a man named Quine. Erdman Quine. I understand he won a mine here in a game of cards.'

'I am Romero and here there are card games. But where did you hear this?'

'In Mesilla. At the Drover's Bar.'

'News travels on the wings of eagles.'

'Quine is with two Anglos. And a woman,' Justin said.

'Ah, the woman,' spoke up the red-bearded man. 'A sight I will not likely forget.'

'Are they at the mine?' Justin demanded.

'Maybe.' The man squinted at Justin. 'I don't favor Quine or his methods. And there's some talk he used fancy cards to fleece Romero's cousin out of the mine, but—'

'Where can I find the mine?'

'But Quine, with all his faults,' the red-bearded man went on, 'is now one of us. He's taking ore from God's good earth. He's not a cowman, who screams to heaven just because a blade of precious grass might be lost when a claim is staked.'

Romero put two large brown hands flat on the bar top and leaned toward Justin. 'Without mines this place is nothing. I warn my cousin many times to not play cards when he is drunk. But when he is drunk he has the temper of a snake. Maybe come spring he get his mine back. Who knows? Until then, you stay away. *Sabe?*'

'I'll find that mine if I have to ride every square mile of these mountains,' Justin said coldly.

'You should've stayed in Texas, Mr. Emery.'

The voice was deep, faintly amused, coming from behind Justin. He spun, putting his back to the bar. Not ten feet away stood the big man who had attacked him so senselessly at Hearn's Store in Mexia.

Charlie Ivory had come in quietly, tracking fresh mud over old on the board floor. Men swung their heads to stare at the towering figure. An uneasy silence ran through the room.

'He's been askin' about your friend Quine,' said a man.

'I'm in luck,' Justin breathed, staring at Ivory. 'You're the one to take me to Quine.'

'You got no luck at all, Emery.' Charlie Ivory laughed, and began pulling heavy gloves from his hands.

'Don't bother taking them off,' Justin told

him. 'You're going back into the cold again.' Turning his body so his right arm was away from the bar, Justin swept aside the tail of his coat.

Before he could reach his holstered revolver, Romero lunged across the bar top. The Mexican caught Justin's right arm in his two hands.

'Red!' Romero yelled at the red-bearded man. 'Get his gun. He don't shoot my place all to hell, by damn.'

Off balance, Justin pivoted, trying to pull free of Romero. The red-bearded one had already snapped the revolver from under Justin's coat.

Romero clung to the arm doggedly. As Justin was about to be pulled the rest of the way across the bar, Romero turned him loose.

The sudden release of his arm threw Justin off balance again. He reeled, tripped over a cuspidor, stumbled straight into the barn-plank solidity of Charlie Ivory's chest. Laughing, Ivory sidestepped, put out a foot. Justin started falling. As he went down, Ivory clubbed him on the neck.

Justin struck the floor with his forehead, only half able to break the fall with his elbows. Dazed, he rolled aside and blinked up at the hand-hewn beams of the ceiling.

Charlie Ivory removed his coat and said, 'Romero, keep a gunnysack handy. I figure to use it to carry Justin Emery's head up to the mine, to let that yellow-haired wife of his get a good look at it.'

'His wife!' exclaimed a man, turning to stare.

Charlie Ivory suddenly had had enough of Quine's tight little hell he'd fashioned up here in the mountains. Them all under the one roof. And at night—sheer torture for a man. Even Kelso Kane, who usually was steady fingered and mean enough to braid the rope for his own hanging, was afraid to move in on her, because they both knew Erd Quine was just waiting for one of them to splinter under the strain of the woman's nearness. Erd would laugh when he pulled the trigger.

Charlie Ivory stood there in the center of the big room looking like a muddied, angry bear. Men had left the stove to line both sides of the cleared space in front of the bar, where Justin lay on the floor. Other men, drawn by shouts from the door that there was a Sunday fight at Romero's, began to stream in, excitement on their faces.

Ivory came to stare down at Emery. He'd tried to be nice to Samantha, but she treated him as if he were a sack of garbage. She would rarely speak, just give him that ice-blue stare with her eyes.

'She was married to Emery here,' Charlie Ivory said through his teeth. 'Then she run off with Erd Quine.'

'Against her will!' cried Justin, and managed

to get to his knees.

'She's nothing but a—'

'You won't slander her!' Justin flung himself forward, his arms locking about Ivory's knees. Ivory crashed to the floor, his two hundred and forty-five pounds shaking the walls. But he was instantly on his feet, his lips twisted in a snarl. He'd lost his hat. Long hair curved down either side of his face.

'So you aim to fight, Mr. Emery,' he said, pleased. 'This I like. This I like fine. You got out of it once at Mexia. You won't get out of this.'

He sprang forward, but Justin twisted aside. Ivory slammed into a deal table. It splintered under his weight. He rose, snatching a smashed chair leg. Holding it like a club, he lunged, tried to brain Justin. Justin pulled away, heard the club whistle past his ear. He closed quickly, before Ivory could wheel and get set again. Justin's lifted knee drove deep into the big man's midsection. Ivory's breath whistled and he dropped the club.

Sensing victory, Justin brought up his right. But Ivory suddenly grabbed him, ducking the blow. He locked both arms around Justin's waist. They wrestled their way across the room, scattering onlookers, overturning chairs.

'Ivory'll kill him!' somebody cried.

'I don't favor a man who'll slander a woman!' shouted the red-bearded one. 'Whip him, Emery. I'm for you now!'

199

CHAPTER TWENTY-FIVE

Desperately Justin tried to pry his way out of Ivory's crushing grip at his waist. But Ivory slowly bent him backward, increasing the pressure across Justin's spine. Justin clubbed him about the head. But with his chin buried against Justin's chest, Ivory presented a poor target.

Each time Justin tried to use his body for leverage to swing Ivory off balance, the big man shifted his feet, countering the move. Justin tried to bring up a knee. It only scraped Ivory's thigh.

At the instant Justin thought surely his spine would snap, he abruptly ceased to struggle. He hung in Ivory's grip like a dead weight. For an instant Ivory was pulled off balance, and the hands behind Justin's back unlocked to spring apart to break the fall. They crashed to the floor together, with Justin bringing up the heel of his hand into Ivory's nose. Ivory screamed at the pain. Before Justin could get out from under him, blood from the ruined nose spurted across his shirt.

Staggering to his feet, Justin stood for a moment, head down. Somehow he managed to get out of his heavy coat so he'd have more freedom of movement. He tried to breathe the overheated air that was smudged with tobacco smoke. Before his eyes swam the excited faces of the onlookers. Some of them shouted encouragement; others yelled for Ivory to get up and finish it.

At bay, Ivory climbed slowly to his feet and glared at Justin. Dragging a dirty bandana from his pocket, he wiped blood from his face.

'Emery,' he said, breathing hard, 'now I aim to kill you. I aim to stomp you to pieces.'

This was greeted with a dead silence. A gust of wind whipped at a loose board on the roof. The men stared at Ivory, now stowing the bloodied bandana in a hip pocket. They looked at the large boots with the heavy heels that Ivory bragged would be the instruments of murder. Then they shifted their eyes to Justin Emery.

Justin threw his coat across the bar. Romero still stood behind it, his brown face impassive. 'You could have kept out of it,' Justin panted.

Romero shrugged. '*Si*, I could have.' And in that moment Justin sensed a faint regret in the Mexican's voice. But he did not have time to dwell on this.

Ivory rushed him again.

Justin tried to move out of the way. His legs felt heavy, and his breath was short. It was too soon after his ordeal at Princess Station for him to be trying to match blows with a man the size of Charlie Ivory.

They slugged each other, their fists making blunt and ugly sounds. Justin tasted the metallic bite of his own blood, as a fist smashed the underside of a cheek against his teeth.

They broke apart. Ivory came in again with such force that his shoulder sent Justin reeling into the crowd. Hands picked Justin up. Twisting aside, he tried to snatch a gun from one of the onlookers to end this stupidity. Couldn't the fools understand that Ivory meant what he said? Were they going to stand by and watch Ivory use his boots?

Before Justin could get his fingers on a gun butt, Ivory seized him around the waist. He made a half turn and sent Justin spinning into one of the center poles that supported the ceiling. Justin crashed into the timber with such force he felt that his ribs must be smashed. Bent at the waist, he gasped for breath.

Ivory came in close and tried to kick him in the face. Even hurt, doubled up as he was, Justin was able to step back. He had presence of mind enough to catch Ivory's swinging foot.

Ivory screamed as Justin twisted hard. 'My ankle!' Ivory managed to kick himself free.

The big man closed in again, ponderous fists swinging. He limped now on the ankle Justin had tried with all his strength to break. Justin stood his ground, took a blow high on the forehead that staggered him. But he was able to deliver two solid smashes to Ivory's face.

202

For a moment Ivory's knees started to cave. But he quickly recovered and Justin's faint hope of victory was gone. They sparred, circled. Suddenly Charlie Ivory lowered his head and rushed. Momentum and sheer strength drove the crown of his head through Justin's guard. His head struck Justin's breastbone with the force of a runaway team.

Under the impact Justin was knocked through the winter swing doors. He came down hard on the boardwalk, built some six feet above the street at this point. He skated across the walk on his shoulderblades, then dropped into the slush of the street. There he lay stunned. Some small boys came running, unmindful of the women who shouted for them to come back.

As Justin tried to pick himself up, the crowd, led by Charlie Ivory, burst through the doors. One of the doors had been partially torn free of its bottom hinge and hung crookedly. Above Justin loomed Ivory, on the edge of the walk. Blood from his smashed nose made Ivory look grotesque.

'Get me a bigger sack, Romero,' he called over his shoulder. 'I'm goin' to take all of Emery home to show her.'

Then he leaped off the edge of the walk. Justin caught a glimpse of the muddied bootheels coming straight down, aimed for his face. Frantically he rolled aside. Ivory came down hard in the slush, his feet shooting out from under him.

On hands and knees, Ivory looked around, blinking his eyes as if the drop into the street had momentarily distorted his vision.

Then his gaze centered on Justin, on his feet now, with the crowd lining the walk above. Others were streaming down from the mill, shouting, laughing. A deadly dull Sunday in the winter mountains, had become not such a waste after all.

Justin stiffened as he saw Ivory set himself. He couldn't stand many more of those rushes. Ivory would wear him down and then, at his leisure, kick him to pieces. Justin's head pounded. He thought of the way this brainless hulk of a man had insulted Samantha. Good God, what was happening to her at the hands of Quine?

Then Ivory was coming for him again. Justin pulled back his head and felt Ivory's knuckles scrape across a cut already open on his cheek. In close, he brought up his right, driving it into Ivory's midriff. When the big man doubled up with a grunt of pain, Justin struck him flush on the jaw. Ivory stumbled, weaved for a moment.

With the crowd yelling, Justin struck repeatedly at Ivory's face. A look of bewilderment dulled the man's eyes. Then the eyes suddenly crossed. Ivory dropped face down into the slush. There he lay, gasping, his hands clawing at the mud and ice and dirty snow. He did not get up.

Justin reeled to the walk, leaned back against the supports. The red-bearded man knelt down and handed him his gun. Justin tried to take it in his right hand, but the fingers refused to respond. The gun slipped through his fingers into the street. He picked it up with his left hand.

'I want his horse,' Justin gasped, straightening up. 'And get me a rope.'

'You aim to hang him?'

'He's taking me to the mine.'

'I'll show you where it is,' Romero said, from the walk.

'Thanks, no,' Justin said through his cut lips. It hurt him to talk. 'I'll find it myself.'

Some of the men boosted Charlie Ivory into the saddle of a Morgan, a stout horse for a large man. They had to hold Ivory in the saddle. He bled over the cantle, and the smell of blood made the big horse edgy. A man brought up Justin's coat and hat. Justin shoved his revolver into his belt. The holster had been torn loose at some point in the fight; he didn't remember when. Justin drew Ivory's rifle from a saddleboot and threw it into the street. There was no revolver at Ivory's belt.

Then Justin got Ivory's rope and threw a loop over his head. Stiffly, wincing at the pain of his hurts, Justin managed to mount his own horse. Tying the rope to the horn, Justin shouted for Charlie Ivory to look around. At last Ivory lifted his head and stared.

Justin said, 'You're taking me to the mine. You try and get away and that rope'll snap your neck like a stick.'

With a swollen finger Ivory felt the noose about his neck. He went a little pale under the scraped places on his face.

One of the men said, 'You're a fool to do this, Emery, the shape you're in.'

'The shape I'm in is just fine for what I have to do.'

While the crowd watched in silence, Charlie Ivory led the way out of town on his Morgan. The skinned knuckles of his left hand bled against the reins he held.

'Maybe we better foller along,' a man suggested.

But he was voted down. 'Leave 'em be,' the red-bearded man said. 'It's Justin Emery's fight. He's done right well so far. I'm wishing him luck for the rest of it.'

CHAPTER TWENTY-SIX

Five miles north of town Ivory left the road and took a steep trail through a canyon. Aspens, gaunt and leafless, dotted the canyon floor. Ivory turned his head, looking back along the rope cinched to the horn of Justin's saddle. 'Cut me loose and go back to Texas,' he said, speaking for the first time since they had left town.

Justin said, 'Keep going.'

'You're a damn fool, Emery.' Ivory's gaze narrowed in the scarred face. 'I seen you favor your right hand. You'll have to use a gun with your left.'

'So I fight left-handed.'

'Damn you, no other man ever whupped me with his fists. If it's the last thing I do, I'll stomp you to pieces. I won't use a gun—that'll be too quick.'

'You don't have a gun,' Justin reminded him crisply.

'Just remember what I said.'

'You do one thing to attract Quine's attention, and I'll open up the back of your head.'

Ivory faced around. The Morgan climbed, grunting at the weight. Ivory's nose had started to bleed again. The big horse seemed uneasy with the odor of blood constantly in its nostrils.

'How much farther?' Justin said, when they were out of the canyon.

'Another mile. Emery, you better think it over. Quine and Kelso will cut you down before you can even draw breath.'

'Can we be seen from the mine as we approach?' Justin asked, knowing there was no reason for Ivory to give him a straight answer.

'We can be seen,' Ivory said. 'Damn right. That's what I been tryin' to tell you. You'll be ridin' right into it.'

'How come you went to town alone?'

'For supplies that I never got.'

'Then there's no reason for Quine to expect trouble. You'll be coming back from town as if nothing is wrong.'

'With a rope around my neck?' Ivory sneered. 'The minute he spots that, you're in trouble.'

'Pray he doesn't spot it until I get close enough to him. Or you'll be the one in trouble.' Then Justin added, 'I imagine Quine's the type who wouldn't mind sacrificing you if it meant he could get at me.'

Ivory, twisted in the saddle, seemed to reflect on this. Justin knew he had made a point. Ivory was chewing it over.

Finally the big man said, 'About twenty yards ahead the trail angles sharp right. It climbs a hump of rock. That's where they can see us from the shack.'

'Hold up here, then,' Justin ordered, and drew rein. He sat his saddle, looking around. To his left were high boulders and shin oak. A thick stand of junipers lined the right side of the trail.

Ivory had brought the Morgan to a halt, with plenty of slack in the rope leading from Justin's saddlehorn to the noose.

'Here's what you do,' Justin said quietly. 'When I give the word, you step down.'

'Then what?'

Justin jerked a thumb at a juniper growing

beside the steep and muddy trail. 'I'm going to tie you and gag you.

And you're going to take it and not open your mouth. If you make one move to get away, I'm going to finish you.' He paused for breath. 'After the beating you gave me, I'll have no conscience about that.'

Ivory seemed impressed. But Justin knew that the wise thing to do was shoot Ivory and be done with it. In his father's time this would have been done, for a man's life so constantly hung by a thread that any leniency toward an enemy only compounded the risk.

Perhaps the West today would more or less revert to its former savagery, after the trouble brought on by the Great White Ruin. Old values quickly dissolved under the pressures of bankruptcy. There was no telling what lasting effects the freeze would have on mens' minds or their morals.

Ivory seemed to sense Justin's indecision. When they dismounted, Ivory suddenly sat himself down in the center of the muddy trail. He grinned at Justin defiantly with his broken mouth.

'Go ahead,' he taunted. 'Tie me to the tree, if you think you can.'

'I can and will.'

It pained Justin's right hand to grip the rope and haul back on it. Ivory, pulled off balance, made choking sounds as he fought the tightening noose about his neck. Justin was about to draw his revolver, when he heard a sound.

Stiffening, he looked uptrail. There on the hump of ground stood Samantha and a man with a copper-colored mustache. From descriptions he had heard of the man, Justin knew it to be Erdman Quine. But his eyes at that moment were for Samantha. He remembered how she had stood out above all women present, the first time he had seen her in St. Louis. In that moment he had known that he must have her, no matter what. And he felt the same in this moment deep in the snowy Mogollon Mountains of New Mexico.

She stood tall above him, wearing a brown traveling cloak over her dress. Her pale hair, slicked back, tied with a black ribbon, hung down her back, nearly to her waist. Her face seemed a little drawn, but it was still beautiful, her wide blue eyes clear and steady.

She said quite calmly, 'Justin, what in the world are you doing here?'

At her side, Quine held a rifle. His mustache needed trimming. He wore a hat, on the back of his head, and an open corduroy jacket, pants, and high-laced boots. He seemed to be tremendously amused about something.

'Samantha,' Justin said, 'I've come to take you home.'

She tilted her head, the lovely lips parting. He saw the tip of her tongue move thoughtfully along the full underlip in that provocative way that always stirred him. 'My home is here, with Erd,' she said.

Charlie Ivory started to get up, fumbling with the noose still about his neck. 'Erd, keep a gun on him. I'm goin' to stomp him.'

'Stay right where you are,' Quine snapped. 'It looks as if he beat you. If he did, he's more man than I thought.'

'Erd, goddam it—'

'I should brain you for bringing him here. Now sit right there till I tell you to move.'

Samantha smoothed her hair. 'Yes, it was foolish for Ivory to lead Justin here.' Her shoulders shrugged under the brown coat. 'As long as it's done, maybe it's better this way.'

'Tell Justin Emery how you feel,' Quine said.

'I love my husband, of course.'

'And I'm your husband,' Justin said, turning his body so he could reach the belted revolver with his left hand.

'The divorce wasn't legal,' Samantha said. 'Erd checked on it. I'm still married to him.'

'I see.'

Justin tipped his head slightly so his eyes would be partially screened by his hatbrim. He looked quickly to his right, then to his left. But in the towering boulders and clumps of shin oak he saw no sign of the other one, Kelso Kane. He experienced a cold twitching sensation along his spine.

Quine said, smiling, 'Samantha, tell him

211

about his brother.'

Samantha lowered her eyes. 'It isn't a thing that a woman likes to talk about.'

'The two brothers fought over you,' Quine said. 'Did Justin have a good reason for being suspicious?'

'He was jealous. I suppose he had a right to be.'

'I think you're lying,' Justin said, peering up at them on the rise of ground. He could see no sign of horses. Obviously they had come this far on foot. He knew that somehow he had been seen approaching with Ivory.

'Tell him the rest of it,' Quine said, his voice a little sharper now, the hazel eyes a little less amused. His knuckles were white against the rifle stock and barrel.

'I thought I was in love with Ford,' Samantha said, and Justin noted the tension building at the corners of her mouth.

'You're not elaborating very much,' Quine snapped.

'I was with Ford every time Justin's back was turned.'

'Tell him about the time in Prescott. About McCallum. How you sneaked around with McCallum and how I intended killing him, but somebody else shot him first. And how they said they intended to hang me for it. And how they sent me to Yuma, because my father had been a respected citizen, so they said.' Quine's eyes took on a wildness. 'And they locked me up, intending that never again would I have the comfort of my wife. And while I rotted in that rock and iron trap, another man slept with my wife.'

Samantha swallowed. 'It's all true. Every word. Justin, get on your horse and ride out. Don't ever come back.'

Justin hooked his left thumb in his belt. 'Is this what you want?'

'It is,' she said, peering down. Her eyes moved rapidly to her right and then back. And Justin knew she was trying to tell him something. He guessed what the message meant.

Ivory, sitting on the ground, was looking up at her. 'Erd, she's tryin' to signal him with her eyes.'

'Probably trying to let Emery know that Kelso is back there someplace by now,' Quine said with a hard smile.

'Justin, this is your chance to leave,' Samantha urged, her voice showing strain.

Quine laughed, holding the rifle loosely in his hands. 'Tell Emery the rest.'

'I've told it all,' she said, flicking a glance at Quine.

'About the cattle.'

'Erd, you can't—'

'Emery, you heard her admit her indiscretions. Under the circumstances, do you still want her back?'

'I do.'

213

'I thought so. I figured you right from the first. So now it'll cost you one thousand head of Hayfork cows.'

'Erd, I already told you, I won't be a party—'

'Shut up! Emery, the cattle are to be delivered on the Mexican side of the river at Quintero Crossing.'

'Until we have roundup,' Justin said, 'I'm not sure how many cows survived the blizzard.'

'You have one month,' Quine stated flatly. 'Buy or steal if you don't have enough.' Quine's hand tightened on the rifle. 'I'll keep Samantha until delivery is made.'

Justin shook his head. 'These are civilized times. You can't get away with kidnaping a woman.'

'You bring the law, or you try and back out of the deal in any way, and I promise you, you'll wish I'd killed her.'

Samantha lifted both hands to her face, suddenly cracking. 'Erd, let him go now. Let him ride out. You *promised*!'

Fragments of old prayers his mother had recited by lampglow spun through Justin's mind. He took a deep breath, with his ribs aching. Better to risk her life here and now than to let her remain in the hands of Erd Quine, even for another hour. And even if cattle were delivered, he knew Quine's word was not worth the value of the Jeff Davis dollars in the Major's old trunk back at Hayfork.

On the ground, directly ahead, hands pressed into the mud, sat Charlie Ivory. Unarmed, but dangerous. Somewhere back in the rocks and the shin oak lurched Kelso Kane. Above, at Samantha's side, was Erd Quine, holding a rifle.

CHAPTER TWENTY-SEVEN

At that moment Justin dropped to his knees in the mud. His left hand awkwardly drew the revolver. Samantha screamed.

Instead of remaining on the ground, Charlie Ivory leaped to his feet. He sprang straight at Justin, crying, 'I'm goin' to kick your brains loose!'

In his wild plunge Ivory blocked Justin's target.

Two shots cracked out, Justin's revolver and Quine's rifle. Both shots ripped into Ivory, front and back. He twitched in midair, then came down hard on the slick trail. Quine, sighting his rifle on Justin, was suddenly set upon by Samantha.

Cold sweat drenched Justin's back as he held his fire for fear of hitting her. He tensed his body against the expected blow of Kelso Kane's shot into his spine.

He saw Samantha's fingers locked in the front of Quine's shirt. Angrily, Quine tried to swing her off. One of her hands tore his shirt, baring his chest. He caught her up close, snapping off a one-handed rifle shot at Justin. The hasty shot went into the ground, throwing a gout of mud across one side of Justin's face.

Justin lifted his revolver, saw Samantha clawing at Quine's eyes. With an oath Quine fell back out of sight beyond the hump of ground.

A sound in the rocks alerted Justin. There was the sound of a man plunging through brush, to Justin's left. Leaping to his feet, Justin stumbled as his leg, twisted in the fight with Ivory, started to fold. But he regained his balance.

Gambling that Samantha could keep Quine engaged, Justin turned his back. Kelso Kane clawed his way through a narrow slot between high boulders, trying to reach the trail. The barrel of the revolver he held scraped rock. But he had waited too long to come up behind his quarry.

At that moment he saw Justin and his head snapped up. 'Your Emery luck,' he snarled. 'And I had a chance to shoot you in the back.' Then his mouth twisted bitterly in the long brown face. 'But I figured on watching you and Quine shootin' yourselves to pieces, and me ending up with the woman.'

Kane, partially hidden by high boulders, now emerged from the slot. He fired, the bullet ricocheting off a knob of rock not a foot from Justin's head. The swollen knuckles of Justin's left hand contracted as the trigger finger exerted pressure. Kane was setting himself for another shot when Justin's bullet took him squarely in the face.

Kane rolled into the muddy trail, startling Charlie Ivory's horse. Already edgy and now spooked by the firing, the Morgan swung out of the junipers where it had wandered. It leaped Charlie Ivory's body, heading straight for Justin. But Justin flung himself aside. As he struck the ground he was half turned, so he saw the panicked Morgan trample the skull of Kelso Kane in its wild flight.

Feeling a raw sickness in his throat at the sight, Justin picked himself up. The horse was far down trail now, plunging through shin oak. When Justin turned there was still no sight of Quine or Samantha on the rise of ground.

Desperately, Justin started up the slant, his boots sliding in the mud. Once he almost dropped his revolver. He skirted the body of the big man he had fought so desperately today in Mogollon. When he neared the ridge, with his heart pounding, he heard Samantha's low sobs.

Then he saw them, some twenty feet on the opposite side of the hump of ground. Quine, his clothing muddy, his face bleeding from ugly scratches, had Samantha by the hair. He was dragging her through a crusting of snow.

Something made Quine look up. 'Emery,

you'll have your woman!' he shouted.

Deliberately, he released her hair and aimed the rifle at her head. Justin fired by instinct. His shot struck Quine in the left side before the rifle could be fired. Quine went down, hard. But he fell prone across the rifle.

Justin leaped toward him, trying again to fire. He saw the recoil of the heavy rifle as Quine, despite his cramped position, managed to squeeze off a shot. Justin felt the impact against his chest.

He had a glimpse of clear New Mexican sky, tilting, as he fell. Then darkness.

CHAPTER TWENTY-EIGHT

Justin lay in the makeshift mine hospital at Mogollon. The story told the deputy who came up from Silver City was to the effect that Justin Emery had accidentally shot himself. His wife, Mrs. Justin Emery, could verify that.

'She's the handsome woman tending him over at the hospital,' said a man in Romero's.

'And them three at Las Rosas Mine,' the deputy said suspiciously. 'What about them? I suppose they also shot themselves.'

'No love they have for each other,' said Romero across his bar, as he poured free whisky. 'We all knew that one day they would find reason to shoot each other.'

'Did a damn good job,' the deputy said gruffly. 'Dead, all three of 'em.'

But the deputy left and finally one day Justin opened his eyes. He ached and his mouth tasted of fever. He could scarcely move because his chest was so thickly bandaged. A gray-bearded man looked down, held Justin's wrist.

'Twenty-two years ago I saw men less hurt than you left on a battlefield to die,' the man said. 'You can thank God we've made a little progress since then.'

'I do thank God,' Justin said, his voice sounding strange in his ears. 'My wife—' His gazed roved around the white-walled room.

'Here, Justin.' She came into view to put a hand on his forehead. 'Your fever's down.'

He gripped her hands. 'What happened after I was shot? I've had a hundred nightmares—'

'Later, Justin,' she whispered.

Finally, when they were alone in the room and Justin had gained a little more strength, she told him.

'Erd started crawling toward you. You didn't move and I thought you were dead. But I knew that, even though you had wounded him, Erd could put another bullet in you.' She paused, clenching her hands in her lap.

'Go on, Samantha,' Justin urged.

'But I reached you first and got your revolver. I guess it surprised him. Before he could shoot me, I—' She closed her eyes, stiffening there in the chair beside his bed. 'I'm thankful there was one shot left in your gun.'

'It took nerve to face him that way.'

Her eyes opened and she looked at Justin. 'Now that you're going to be all right, I'll take my leave.'

'Leave?'

'Mexico was my home once. I have friends there.'

'I want you back.'

She shook her head. 'You'd always remember that I went away with him.'

'You did it to keep him from murdering me'

'You'd always remember another thing, Justin, because you're a man.'

'Only the best about you is what I'll remember, because there is nothing else.'

'You'd remember that Erd was once my husband.' She looked at him steadily. 'In Erd's eyes I was still his wife. I didn't have the strength to refuse what was expected of me.'

'It's in the past.'

'Go home, Justin, and forget me. I've brought you nothing but unhappiness.'

'You come home with me, Samantha. It's where you belong. With me.'

There came a knock on the door and Samantha said, 'Come in.' Turning to Justin, she said, 'It's Ford. I sent for him. He's been here for three days now.'

Justin took his hand from under the

blankets. The hand was thin, still bruised from the encounter with Charlie Ivory. He shook hands with his brother.

Ford had lost weight and around his eyes were new lines. 'You scared me, Justin. But I should've known you were the Major's son. Nothing could whip you.'

'You're also the Major's son, Ford.'

Ford sat down on the edge of the bed. 'There's a weak strain in every family. I got a full dose of it.'

'Listen to me, Ford—'

'You and Darsie can bring Hayfork back. I can't. I'd like to sell out my share to you. Pay what you can when you can. I could live on a hundred dollars a month.'

'And what do you plan to do?'

'I saw a lot of California those months I went to school out there. It's a place where I could maybe put down my roots and nobody would know the things I've done.'

'Ford,' Justin said quickly, 'I've forgiven you for that. I should have been man enough to forgive you years ago.'

Ford gave him a tight smile. 'I haven't yet forgiven myself. Maybe that's it.'

'Try California for a year. If it doesn't work out, come home.'

Ford stared down at the hands gripping his knees. 'If I ever did come home,' he said, not looking at Justin, 'I wouldn't be alone.'

'I expect you to marry. Why not? What's so

terrible about that? We could build a new house for you—'

'Justin, you don't understand. It's Ivy. We've talked it over. She says maybe I'm taking a chance. She says maybe she won't be a good wife. But she says she'll try mightily. And I believe she will.'

For a moment Justin was too stunned to speak. Then he said, 'But why, Ford? There are a dozen nice girls in Midpoint.'

Ford stood up. 'I don't figure to argue about it, Justin.'

'But, why?'

'I only want to say this. Maybe it's a way for me to make the score come out a little even.'

'Even?'

'I took the life of one girl with my own foolishness. Maybe I can give life to another.' Ford put on his hat. 'Anyhow, I'm going to try.'

Justin sank deeper into the blankets as Ford stepped toward the door. Then Justin lifted his head. 'I'm not splitting Hayfork again. I did it once. That time I had my mule blood hot, as the Major would say.'

'We'll see, Justin.'

'But I want you to come home. And when you do—bring your wife.'

'Maybe, one day.' Ford shrugged. 'Who knows?' he stepped out, closing the door.

Justin groped for Samantha's hand. 'Maybe he's doing right,' Justin murmured. 'I hope so. But I'm certain of one thing.' With his free

222

hand he gestured toward the door. 'As the Major would say, yonder goes a real man.'

We hope you have enjoyed this Large Print book. Other Chivers Press or G.K. Hall & Co. Large Print books are available at your library or directly from the publishers.

For more information about current and forthcoming titles, please call or write, without obligation, to:

Chivers Press Limited
Windsor Bridge Road
Bath BA2 3AX
England
Tel. (01225) 335336

OR

G.K. Hall & Co.
P.O. Box 159
Thorndike, Maine 04986
USA
Tel. (800) 223-2336

All our Large Print titles are designed for easy reading, and all our books are made to last.